ON
FIRE

ON FIRE

A TEEN WOLF NOVEL

NANCY HOLDER

GALLERY BOOKS   MTV BOOKS

NEW YORK LONDON TORONTO SYDNEY NEW DELHI

Gallery Books
A Division of Simon & Schuster, Inc.
1230 Avenue of the Americas
New York, NY 10020

Text by Nancy Holder

First MTV Books/Gallery Books trade paperback edition June 2012.

GALLERY and colophon are registered trademarks of Simon & Schuster, Inc.

For information about special discounts for bulk purchases,
please contact Simon & Schuster Special Sales at 1-866-506-1949
or business@simonandschuster.com.

The Simon & Schuster Speakers Bureau can bring authors to
your live event. For more information or to book an event
contact the Simon & Schuster Speakers Bureau at 1-866-248-3049
or visit our website at www.simonspeakers.com.

Designed by Akasha Archer

Library of Congress Cataloging-in-Publication Data

Holder, Nancy.
   On fire : a Teen wolf novel / Nancy Holder.
      p.   cm.
   I. Teen wolf (Television program)   II. Title.
   PZ7.H703260n 2012
   [Fic]—dc23
                              2012002504

ISBN 978-1-4516-7447-7
ISBN 978-1-4516-7448-4 (ebook)

Manufactured in the United States of America

10   9   8   7   6   5

Who are you . . . really?

—Mikky Ekko

CHAPTER ONE

I t was the night of the parent-teacher conferences at Beacon Hills High, and everyone in the school parking lot was panicking. A wild animal was racing up and down the rows of parked cars. Scott McCall could hear it growling; when he focused his werewolf vision, he could see flashes of it as it slunk along, stalking warm prey. People ran, leaped into their cars, didn't look where they were going. Someone backed into Sheriff Stilinski and he fell down, hard enough to make it impossible for him to get to his ankle holster.

Then Allison's father shot twice.

And it was over.

Scott kept Allison in his sights as they joined the circle forming silent witness to the execution. On the ground lay a mountain lion—*the* mountain lion that everyone had been blaming for all the brutal deaths in Beacon Hills, a small California town. But Scott knew it had done nothing to deserve this. It hadn't even wandered onto school grounds of its own accord.

It had been lured.

And the deaths would not end.

Somewhere out there, the real culprit was watching. Gloating. The Alpha, the werewolf that had bitten Scott and cursed him, was still at large, still free to kill.

Allison looked up at Scott, her big brown eyes wide, lips pressed together. Her long brown curls hung over the shoulders of her black leather jacket as she wrapped her arms around herself. Then she gave another pitying look at the mountain lion, the folds of her green and blue scarf brushing against her chin. No one was cheering the death of the animal, least of all her. Scott smelled her dismay, heard her pounding heartbeat. He would have done anything to keep her safe tonight. He was relieved beyond telling that he hadn't shifted in all the stress.

She was still safe from his terrible secret.

Narrowing his eyes at Scott, Allison's father put a hand on her shoulder. Chris Argent was the leader of the werewolf hunters, and he had shot Scott through the arm with a crossbow bolt the very first night Scott had shifted. Derek had rescued Scott and told him about the hunters. It had been a terrible shock when Scott had discovered that Mr. Argent was also Allison's father. So far, though, Mr. Argent hadn't realized that Scott was the werewolf he had nearly caught just a few short weeks before.

Now, in the parking lot, Allison took one last look at Scott, as if she were memorizing what he looked like, and then father and daughter walked toward Allison's car. Mr. Argent opened the passenger side door and Allison got in. Obviously he was going to drive her car home, and Allison's mom would take their SUV back to their house. As Mr.

Argent shut the car door, he turned and gave Scott a last, long, hard, so-very-pissed-off stare. But it was only the look of a protective father angry with a boy for encouraging his daughter to ditch school.

We're so busted, Scott thought.

It was not the perfect ending he had imagined for the perfect birthday for Allison. It was just that she'd looked so stricken when all those balloons from Lydia had floated out of her locker this morning. Scott hadn't even known it was her birthday. Turned out she hated celebrating her birthday at school. Scott hadn't known Allison was seventeen, a year older than the other kids in their class—older than *him*— and didn't want anyone to know. It was because of all the moving around. But people in other towns had assumed all kinds of things—that she was dumb, that she'd had a baby.

He'd wanted to protect her from a day like that. So they'd taken off. And the day had been magical. Once darkness had fallen, she'd said she never wanted it to end. And then she'd told him that she wished she could spend the night with him.

With me, Scott thought, his own heartbeat picking up, a thrill rushing through him even now, as his mom gave him the evil eye and muttered, "In the car. *Now*."

He let her march on ahead, like a hangman leading him to the gallows. Her back was ramrod straight, her shoulders raised. Everything about her spoke of her intense disappointment in him. She was really mad, and he didn't blame her. In addition to skipping school, he'd blown off their parent-teacher conference, so blissed out to be with Allison that he'd forgotten all about it. Just as he'd been forgetting about school, too. He was flunking chemistry and he had no grades higher than a C. Finding out he was a werewolf and being with Allison took up all his attention.

His mom got behind the wheel and he buckled up. Unlike so many other drivers, she was careful starting the car and pulling out of the lot. As they merged onto the street, it started to rain and she flipped on the windshield wipers. One of the wipers squealed against the glass. They needed to be replaced. Their car was falling apart, like their house. He knew his dad wasn't keeping up with the child support payments. Not that his mom had ever mentioned it.

Having werewolf-enhanced senses was a mixed blessing. Sometimes you heard things you'd really rather not know.

At the moment, he was listening to his mom's heartbeat. It hadn't slowed. Maybe tomorrow people would be relieved that the mountain lion had been killed, but tonight, the freakiness of having a supposedly man-killing animal slinking up and down the maze of cars was just too much.

"I'm just so angry at you, Scott. How could you do this?" she said, as they pulled up in front of their house and the car rolled to a stop.

Then she sighed, turned off the car, and gave him a look. Before he could say anything, she got out. The rain pounded down on his head as he got out, too. Walking quickly, he looked around, wondering if the Alpha had followed them and was lurking in the shadows. Stalking him. Creeped out, soaked to the skin, he dashed into the house.

Making sure the door was locked, he braced himself for a lecture, but his mom went straight to her bedroom and shut the door. He headed for his own room. He could hear the rain dripping into the bucket in the bathroom. They had a leaky roof. And leaky pipes. And the furnace needed replacing.

He went to his room and tried to video chat with Stiles, but his best friend wasn't online. Stiles's parent-teacher conference had probably gone a lot better than his own, even if you counted Stiles's ADHD. He wasn't blowing off his classes and getting D pluses on assignments.

He texted Allison, but she didn't answer. For all he knew, her parents had confiscated her phone and her dad would be the one to read his message. Better not to push his luck.

Scott powered down his computer. He was so amped he did some chin-ups and push-ups; then he took a shower, brushed his teeth, and climbed into bed.

That mountain lion didn't do jack, he thought. *And Allison Argent wants to sleep with me.*

Smiling faintly, he bunched his pillow under his head and turned over on his side . . .

. . . rolling onto a pile of leaves. He was shirtless, wearing only his boxers.

Scott lifted his head and sniffed the air. Smoke.

Fire!

He bolted upright. His bare feet sank into wet leaves as he scrabbled to his feet. He sniffed again, trying to figure out where the fire was. There was so much smoke. Animal panic threatened to overtake his human mind. But he kept it together, getting his bearings. An outcropping of rock, the indentation where he had lain. He had awakened here before—the very first time he had gone sleepwalking.

After the Bite.

Ash floated down; the smoke was getting thicker, and Scott heard the crackling of burning wood. He heard a strange whoosh and looked up. The tops of the towering pines had burst into flames that rocketed toward the moon.

The huge, full, bloodred moon.

Full moon, *he thought.* That can't be right.

Coughing, Scott jogged forward as tree after tree caught fire, as if they were chasing him. Closing in.

A growl ripped from his chest and his eyesight shifted, everything going as red as the fire. He saw things moving, shifting. Animals fleeing the flames. Heat prickled his naked shoulders and the backs of his legs. Embers floated down and one landed on his chest. As he brushed it away, he lost his footing on the damp leaves and fell hard onto his back. His breath was knocked out of him, and his thoughts shot to his inhaler. He didn't have it with him. Smoke was pouring over him like someone throwing a blanket over his face. He couldn't breathe; he was out of air, and he was a severe asthmatic.

I'm going to die! *he thought.*

Had been an asthmatic, *he reminded himself. Past tense.*

Before the Bite. Becoming a werewolf had cured him of his life-long asthma.

An enormous, fiery limb broke from the tree above him and plummeted downward like a bomb. He rolled to the side and leaped to his feet. Another branch crashed to his right, sending up sparks.

He was driven forward, coughing hard, his eyes watering. Then, just like the night he had been bitten, a herd of panicked deer burst through the trees, leaping in a distressed stampede around him, at him, over him. As before, one knocked him hard and rolled end over end over end down the hill. Balls of flame careened down the incline at him, as if someone had torched a dozen tumbleweeds and aimed them at him.

Then he hit a tree trunk and pushed up against it. Reaching for a limb, he hoisted himself up, then raised his legs as the balls of fiery brush slammed into the trunk, mere inches beneath him. Sparks skittered upward. His stomach muscles ached, but he held the position. Then the treetop exploded into flame. The heat singed his hair, crackled in his ears.

He dropped down, stamping out the tinderbox of leaves and twigs under his bare feet. His soles blistered and stung.

He began to walk up the hill.

Dead ahead, two red eyes glowed like hellfire itself. Surrounded by darkness, they bored right into his. He could feel the pull of that gaze. Sense the power, the rage behind it.

Come to me, a voice said inside Scott's mind. Commanding, insistent. He didn't want to obey, but he found himself moving forward like a sleepwalker.

Come with me, the voice ordered him.

A tree crashed right in front of Scott, sending up huge clods of dirt and a shower of burning leaves that barely missed him. Then a wall of fire roared up, creating an inferno between him and those eyes. And still Scott climbed toward them, unable to stop himself, heading for certain death. Into hell itself.

And then the voice said:

Kill with me.

"No, I won't!" Scott yelled, bolting upright.

He came to half naked in the forest, alone, halfway up

the hill. He was wearing his boxers, and there was no fire. The trees stood tall and silent, dew clustering on their needles. Lavender painted the sky with the colors of early morning, and in the distance, a bird chirped. Something rustled in the bushes at his feet; a squirrel, maybe, or a rabbit.

Scratching his chest, he pushed his hair out of his eyes and got to his feet with an antsy feeling of déjà vu. He hated this sleepwalking thing, waking up after a blackout to find himself miles away from home, deep inside Beacon Hills Preserve. He never had any memory of how he'd gotten here . . . or of what he'd done before he'd come to. This morning was no different.

Did I do it? he wondered.

Derek Hale, the other Beta werewolf in Beacon Hills, promised him that sooner or later, he was going to kill someone. Derek was in his midtwenties, and he'd been born a werewolf. He'd lived here when he'd been in high school, and his entire family, except for his sister and his uncle, had died in a house fire six years ago. He'd left. Now he was back, lured to Beacon Hills to find his sister—the murdered jogger Stiles had heard about on his father's police scanner the night before school started. Laura Hale.

Scott was a young werewolf, with just one full moon since his Bite, still resisting the call of the Alpha as best he could. He'd already refused to kill with the Alpha once, but Derek said it was only a matter of time before the Alpha forced him to hunt, and to butcher. Scott's only hope was to help Derek find the Alpha first, and kill him.

And if Scott dealt the killing blow himself, he would be free of the werewolf curse. Or so Derek had told him.

But I'm not a killer, he thought as he began to stagger through the forest. The rustling in the bush grew louder, a bit more frantic, and Scott cocked his head, listening, sniffing.

At his feet, stamped into the damp earth, was the print of a single, perfect wolf claw. He bent down and laid his hand over it.

Not mine, he told himself. But he didn't change into a wolf exactly. Derek didn't, either. But Derek's dead sister, Laura Hale, had. Scott and Stiles had seen her in wolf shape when they had dug her up beside the burned-out shell of the Hale family home a few days after school had started. Then they had removed the wolfsbane circling her grave, and she'd been a girl again. A dead girl.

Half of a dead girl.

Scott became aware of something watching him, and he tensed. His fingernails lengthened into claws and he quietly growled.

Slowly he raised his head. His eyesight wolfed, then became human again, as twenty feet away, a beautiful silvery wolf stared calmly at him with yellow eyes. The rising sun cast a glow around it, almost as if it were a magical creature, and it stood statue-still. Scott wondered if he was still dreaming.

Then the wolf turned and trotted gracefully away, slipping among the trees.

School.

"Hey, Scott," Stiles called from the parking lot of Beacon

Hills High as Scott chained his bike and took off his helmet. Before the Bite, Scott's three main goals in life had been playing first line in lacrosse, getting a girlfriend, and buying a car. Accomplishing two out of three was excellent, but he wished he'd put *and stay human* on his list. Funny how it seemed a little more important than getting his own wheels.

"Stiles, I had another weird dream last night," Scott said, as Stiles loped up to him and they walked shoulder to shoulder into the school. Stiles had on his bull's-eye T-shirt, and it kind of freaked Scott out when he wore it. As if it meant that Stiles was a target. They both knew the Alpha wanted Scott to kill with him, to cement Scott's acceptance that he was a member of the Alpha's pack. Who better to take down than the guy Scott's mom had once referred to as his "litter mate"?

"Dream? Did you wake up in the woods?" Stiles asked him. "With rabbit breath?"

"*God*. No." Scott grimaced. "At least, I don't think so. But there was a fire, and—"

"Fire. Which is a recurring theme in the drama that has become your life," Stiles said, aping Scott's grimace. "And we know that this is because—"

"Hi, Scott," Allison said, bobbing over with a worried expression on her face. She was wearing that black-and-purple top with no sleeves and the heeled boots, and she gave him a kiss on the lips right there in front of the whole school, which was *awesome*.

"Catch you later, Bugs," Stiles said, shoving off.

For a second Scott thought he might pass out from the sheer amazingness of Allison's kiss. But her beautiful face was filled with even more concern than Stiles's not-as-beautiful face had been, and he focused hard on what she was saying through his kiss-induced stupor.

" . . . *missing*," she was saying. "He wasn't at his house last night, and Lydia found an odd note in his dresser drawer," she told him. "And his Porsche wasn't in the garage."

Lydia. Porsche. His mind parsed what she was saying, and alarm bells went off. They were talking about Jackson Whittemore. Who was missing—the morning after Scott had had a blackout. He felt queasy.

"Wait. Lydia was at his house but he wasn't?" Scott asked.

"Yeah. His parents are out of town," Allison said, and she had the strangest look on her face. He didn't know how to read it. Was she embarrassed? Shy? Something else?

Whoa, it is *something else*, he thought, grinning at her. She dimpled. She wished it could have been *them* in a house with no parents. Then the bell rang.

"I have to scoot," she said, and gave him another kiss.

Then Lydia passed by, looking exhausted and worried, and Scott swallowed back his dread.

I didn't kill anyone last night, he told himself. *I'd know it if I had.*

But would he?

CHAPTER TWO

At lunch, Allison and Lydia waved Scott over to their usual spot in the cafeteria. It was still so strange to him that he and Stiles sat at the cool table now because Allison and Lydia were friends, and no one was cooler than Lydia Martin—except for Jackson, the captain of the lacrosse team, and Lydia's boyfriend. Who totally had it in for Scott.

And is missing, Scott thought fearfully.

"I told Lydia you'd help us," Allison said as he put his tray on the table and sat down.

"Sure. With what?"

"Finding Jackson," Allison replied.

The four of them were alone for the moment. Despite her perfect makeup and every strand of strawberry blond hair in place, Lydia looked as if she hadn't slept at all. She still looked great—not as great as Allison, but no one was as pretty as Allison—and she glanced furtively around and kept her voice low, talking fast.

"So, I went over to Jackson's like we planned, after the parent-teacher conferences," Lydia said. "His parents had already left for the airport. Paris," she elaborated. "I swear, those people don't have any imagination. They go to Paris all the time. Anyway, he wasn't there. But this was."

She reached into her purse and moved around whatever it was that girls kept in their purses—Scott wasn't exactly clear on that—and pulled out a folded piece of paper, ripped at the bottom. She handed it to Allison, who shared it with Scott.

He looked over her shoulder and read:

Dear Jackson, as you are now called,

My name is Hunter Gramm, and I'm a private detective. I have important information about your birth parents to share with you. To show you that I'm sincere, please look at the enclosed. And then call me at

The rest of the paper was gone, just like Jackson.

"It had to be a phone number," Lydia said. "And I'm thinking a picture of his biological parents. Or maybe a baby picture or adoption papers."

"We think Jackson went to meet him," Allison said, glancing at Lydia, who nodded. "And he hasn't come back."

Scott handed back the note. "And . . . have you contacted Sheriff Stilinski?" The sheriff was Stiles's dad. Scott wouldn't be a werewolf now if Stiles hadn't eavesdropped on his father's call from the department, informing him that a dead jogger had been found in the woods. Make that *half* of a dead jogger. Scott and Stiles had gone out to look for it, too, and that's when the Alpha had attacked him.

"No," Lydia said quickly, "I *haven't* contacted Sheriff Stilinski, and I'm not going to. It might be nothing. And if it's nothing . . ." She moved her shoulders.

"Lydia told her parents she was spending the night at my house last night," Allison said, her cheeks reddening. She cleared her throat. Scott wondered what kind of punishment Allison had gotten for bailing on school the day before. He doubted they'd be spending the night together anytime soon.

"Besides, Jackson is the captain of the lacrosse team," Lydia said. "If it's nothing, it will make him look stupid."

And Coach might demote him, Scott thought, but he sincerely doubted that could actually happen.

Allison handed the paper back to Lydia, and Lydia carefully folded it back up and put it into her purse. Then she pulled out her phone.

"I can access the Where's My Phone app from my phone if I have his user name and password, but I don't . . . seem to know his password at the moment," Lydia said. She made a face. "It's not what it used to be."

Scott was clueless. *"Lydia,"* Allison whispered softly. "That's what the password currently . . . isn't."

Lydia huffed. "Let's not overshare," she said to Allison. She typed in some text on her phone. "I've been trying all kinds of possibilities, and I was wondering if maybe he's using a lacrosse term. I've tried *baller, cannon, man up* . . . "

Allison's brows rose slightly in amusement, and Scott was about to translate what the terms meant when she picked up a french fry off her plate and fed it to him. As he chewed, she rested her head in her arms, cocked her head, and smiled up at him. It was the best-tasting fry in his life *ever.*

"Can you think of anything Jackson would use for a password?" Allison asked Scott.

Other than "JerksRme"? Scott thought, but did not say.

"Oh, don't ask Scott," Lydia said as she stared down at her phone and blew air out her cheeks. "Okay, not 'A stick,' either." She glanced at Allison. "He and Jackson barely know each other."

"They're on the same team," Allison pointed out.

"Hardly." Lydia favored Allison with a pitying smile.

Allison pursed her lips and was about to say something when Stiles arrived, followed by Danny and some of Jackson's and Lydia's other regulars.

"Hey, where's Jackson?" Danny asked. "We were supposed to get together this morning for scrimmage."

"He's not here," Lydia said firmly as she put the note and her cell phone back into her purse and snapped it shut.

"Yeah, but where is he?" he persisted.

Scott took note. Danny was Jackson's best friend, but it was obvious Jackson hadn't told him about the detective or the note. Scott and Stiles told each other just about everything, and Scott was glad of that. Stiles was the only person on the planet who knew that he had become a werewolf.

Well, Derek knew, too, but Derek hardly counted as an actual person. Given a choice between hanging out with Jackson Whittemore or Derek Hale, Scott would have to go with Jackson. Except, of course, that Derek could keep Scott alive—or so he claimed—while Jackson would probably be a little bit psyched if Scott bit the big one.

Hey, I cracked a werewolf joke, Scott thought.

"Jackson is not here," Lydia replied, enunciating carefully, as if Danny might be having trouble understanding her. That was definitely the signal not to pursue the subject. After all, in the boyfriend-girlfriend rules according to Lydia, Jackson should keep her informed of his whereabouts at all times. It would embarrass her to have to admit that she didn't know where he was, either. And no one embarrassed Lydia Martin, ever.

So the subject was dropped. Lunch without Jackson—that was pretty sweet. Even sweeter, Allison fed Scott some more french fries and smiled her little smile, and texted him a happy face.

Life—despite it being life as a werewolf—was good.

Allison couldn't stop thinking about how cute Scott had looked eating her lunch, and she kept daydreaming about doing something with him after school today—it was Friday, glorious Friday—until she remembered that she was grounded. Her father had totally lit into her, pacing and demanding to know how she could have skipped school and gone into the woods while a mountain lion had been on the loose. Her mom had been angry, too, but Allison could tell that if it had been left up to her, she wouldn't have been as harsh about having to stay in all weekend. Her mom liked Scott.

So, score one for my lacrosse guy, she thought. *I've never skipped school before, but I've never had a boyfriend before, either. And I've never had such a perfect birthday. It was worth it. Except I won't get to spend time with Scott except at school until I'm, oh, 112.*

The last bell rang and she headed for her locker, anticipating a less-than-thrilling weekend of homework and hopefully jogging with Aunt Kate. At the thought of her aunt, who was practically more like a sister, she touched her new necklace, the one with the strange creature on it. Kate had given it to her for her birthday.

Then she spotted Lydia waiting for her at her locker. Lydia had on her cute high-waisted coat and a beret.

"I figured out the password," Lydia announced. With an air of triumph, she showed Allison the screen of her smartphone. "It's 'Captain.' And here's where Jackson is."

Allison squinted at the address and phone number on the faceplate as she twirled her combination lock. "He's at a motel?"

Lydia nodded, her expression cool and collected. Allison didn't know what to make of that.

"It appears so. But I've called his phone and he's not picking up. And I called the motel and they haven't seen anyone named Jackson, or who even looks like Jackson. And there's no Hunter Gramm registered."

She peered through her lashes at Allison, who opened her locker and put her lab notebook into her leather messenger bag. Allison smiled uncertainly back, not sure what Lydia was driving at.

"Color me unsurprised," Lydia said. At Allison's confused expression, she explained, "Unsurprised that there's no one there by the name of Hunter Gramm. At this kind of motel, people go by John Smith and Jane Doe. Or possibly Bambi von Boob Job."

Allison blinked at her in horror.

"And pay by the hour," Lydia added.

"No way." She closed her locker door and leaned against it. "Why would a detective arrange to meet Jackson there? And would Jackson even go into a place like that? Wait. Don't answer that."

"Well, apparently his phone did," Lydia said, dropping her facade that the conversation they were having was anywhere close to normal. "I need to check it out." She looked less than thrilled. "Come with me?"

Allison blanched. "I'm grounded," she said quickly. And gratefully. "I can't go anywhere."

"Except maybe my house?" Lydia asked, smiling hopefully. "To work on our English project?"

That we don't have, Allison translated. She licked her lips. "I guess it's worth a shot to at least ask my folks if I can." She'd never been grounded before. She didn't know how it worked. Scott, no, but a girlfriend, yes?

"Thank you," Lydia said.

Just as Allison pulled out her phone, she caught sight of Scott. He was talking to Stiles, his quirky best friend, but he was staring at her. Her insides went all warm and tingly and she gave him a little smile. He grinned and started walking over. Stiles came, too. That was okay with her. She liked Stiles.

"What's up?" Scott asked. "Did you find Jackson?"

"Possibly," Lydia replied, raising her chin. She gave Allison a look. "And about that? We could use some backup," she declared.

"Yeah, um," Allison said anxiously, smiling uncertainly up at him. "Do you want to go to a motel with me?"

• • •

Scott gaped at Allison. *Did she really just ask me to go to a motel?*

He looked over at Stiles for confirmation. Yes, there it was: his best friend's jaw practically dragging on the floor. Stiles looked from Scott to Allison to Lydia and back to Scott, as if asking someone, anyone, in turn to validate this man-dream come true.

"Are you seriously asking me that question?" Scott asked Allison, and she playfully batted his arm.

"Not to do . . . *that*," she said. "We're looking for—"

"We're going on an errand," Lydia cut in, then licked her lips and cleared her throat, as if she had just realized how that might sound.

"I could totally help with that," Stiles said quickly. "Errands are my middle name. Actually, my middle name is almost as difficult to pronounce as my first name, but hey, I could do it."

Lydia slid Stiles a glance that hovered somewhere between incredulous and impatient, and he went silent. Which, Scott knew, could be very challenging for his hyperactive best friend. But it had been achieved before, and could be again if the stakes were high enough. And for Stiles, who had been crushing on Lydia Martin since kindergarten, pleasing her was sky-high stakes.

"Stiles is quite the hacker," Allison said, and Lydia's disdainful gaze grew thoughtful.

"And I'm sure you're very good at tracing people via their phones," Lydia said.

"They have an app for that," Stiles said. "Several, actually." Lydia smiled. "Which, I'm guessing by your expression, you already knew." Scott could see the lightbulb go on. "And this *someone* might be at a motel," Stiles continued. "And I am guessing that this someone might be Jackson."

Lydia shrugged. Then she turned to Allison. "Tell you what. If the boys are willing to go to the motel for us—"

"To a motel. To look for a guy," Stiles said. "Maybe you should ask Danny." Danny, their lacrosse team goalie, was gay, out, and proud. "He could act, you know, more casual about it."

Then Scott shut his eyes against the pain as reality came crashing down on him. "We can't go. We have lacrosse practice."

Stiles stared at him, looking even more dumbfounded than when Allison had asked Scott to go to the motel with her. He gave his head a little shake, then gestured for Scott to move out of earshot of the girls.

As soon as they were a few feet away, he punched Scott in the arm. "Are you *insane?*" he said. "Let's think this through. Getting smacked around by sweaty guys with sticks. Going to a *motel* with a girl."

Scott grinned. "When you put it that way . . ."

"I'll tell the coach you've got food poisoning." Stiles held up his hand as if solemnly swearing to tell the full truth, nothing but the truth, and utter BS. "I'll tell him you're dying."

"If her father finds out, he'll kill me," Scott said.

"He's already trying to kill you. So no worries," Stiles replied cheerfully.

Scott's grin widened. Then it shrank a little. "Yeah, okay, but it looks like it's not just me and Allison going. It's me, Allison, and Lydia."

"And is there any justice in that?" Stiles said with a sigh. He clapped Scott on the shoulder. "Go, my friend, go be a man. I'll take one for the team." Then he glanced longingly in Lydia's direction, sighed again, and took off toward the boys' locker room.

When Scott returned to the girls, Lydia was reapplying her lip gloss and Allison was looking kind of guilty and a little nervous as she held her phone to her ear. Seeing Scott in her makeup mirror, Lydia said to his reflection, "So it occurs to me that I have tons of math homework, and I was wondering if you two could handle the trip to the motel on your own."

She popped the cap back onto her lip gloss and turned around to allow Scott to admire her. Her lips were very shiny. "I'll go camp out at Jackson's, in case he shows."

"Okay, sure. Thanks, Mom," Allison said into the phone. She disconnected. "They said okay." Her forehead was furrowed, as if okay was a bad thing. Scott remembered that she'd been grounded. He had, too, but he was on the honor system. He had lacrosse practice, and his mom had the night shift. They wouldn't be home at the same time until tomorrow morning. Which meant that he could sneak around if he needed to.

"So you can go," Lydia translated, and Allison nodded. Lydia mimicked putting a phone to her ear. "You let me know what you and Scott find out the minute you get there," she ordered Allison.

"I'll call you. Promise," Allison said.

Lydia took off, and Allison and Scott walked to the parking lot. By the time they'd reached her car, she was still looking weirded out, and Scott paused beside the door.

"Is this okay with you?" he asked her.

"Yeah," she said, relaxing a little as she slid her arms around his waist. "It's just . . . I didn't expect my parents to say I could go to Lydia's. Last night my father said I would be grounded until the end of time, and today he seemed almost *glad* that I wasn't coming home."

"Oh." Scott didn't know what to make of that, and it worried him a little. Maybe the Argents were going out werewolf hunting. "But he thinks you're going to Lydia's, right?"

She caught her bottom lip between her teeth, lowered her head, and nodded. She didn't like lying to her parents. He knew how that felt. He hated lying to her.

"Yeah," she said. "He thinks that first we're going to study in the library, where we're not allowed to have cell phones on. And then, he, um, thinks I'm spending the night at her house." She gazed up at him mischievously with those huge dark brown eyes of hers, and he thought he would explode. He still couldn't quite believe that of all the guys in school, Allison Argent had picked him to be her boyfriend.

"So aren't you?" he asked her. "Spending the night at her house?"

She wrinkled her nose, half shy, half flirty. "Maybe not," she replied.

CHAPTER THREE

Stiles suited up and hit the field. Coach Finstock's black hair was wild and free, his gray eyes blazing, and he was taking roll while bellowing out warm-ups. He saw Stiles and said, "Where's McCall?"

"He had to go home, Coach," Stiles said, eyes wide and innocent. "Food poisoning."

The coach did a double take. "What? He makes first line and then he takes a day off on account of a little food poisoning? Where's the team spirit in *that*?"

"He's really sick," Stiles replied, keeping the innocence vibe flowing. He was the king of the "who-me?" fake out, after having trailed after his father on so many of his calls, then pretending not to know any of the gory details. Before the return of Derek Hale to Beacon Hills, local crimes hadn't actually been all that gory. But now that Derek was in town, the ick-o-meter was at full tilt. Coincidence? Stiles thought not.

"Sick," Coach echoed, sounding disgusted.

"Barfing, totally barfing. Everywhere," Stiles confirmed. "Hurling chunks the size of ice cu—"

The coach made a sour face. "Okay, all right, Stilinski. I don't need a picture." He grunted. "Even though I've got one now, thank you very much. Hey." He looked around. "Where's my captain?"

He meant Jackson, of course, and right on cue, Danny, Jackson's best friend, jogged on over.

"He went out of town with his parents, Coach. They cleared it with the office."

"Right, right," Coach Finstock said, nodding. "I remember now. Excused absence. No problem."

Stiles was disgusted. He knew that was a total lie, one planned well in advance. Danny might have not known where Jackson was this morning, but he was playing his part now. Jackson's parents were already out of town, and Lydia had asked Jackson to get out of lacrosse practice so they could get a jump—so to speak—on their weekend alone.

Jackson was the most committed lacrosse player Stiles had ever seen—what players called a "lax-head," but hey, if Lydia crooked her finger Stiles's way, he'd drop out of school if she wanted him to.

Except that Jackson was missing from the party.

And Scott went sleepwalking last night, Stiles thought nervously.

No, no way. Scott had not killed Jackson. There'd be a body.

Unless he ate him all up or something.

"Stilinski, are you going to puke, too?" Coach Finstock asked, peering at him. "Cuz if you think you're going to hurl, you can hit the showers, buddy. We'll do fine without you."

Jackson's little posse of minions snickered and Stiles felt his cheeks go red. Guys like Jackson—rich, athletic—they always got the breaks.

"I'm fine," Stiles insisted.

"Okay, then let's get it moving. And tell McCall one more missed practice and he's benched."

Guys like him and Scott, not so much.

Yet despite my class envy, I hope Scott didn't eat him. Talk about your food poisoning.

"I'll tell him," Stiles said. *And hopefully, he won't be behind bars when I do.*

Hundreds, if not thousands, of fresh bullet holes dotted the charred walls of Derek Hale's family home. Amazingly, it was still standing after Kate Argent had let loose inside with a submachine gun the day before. She'd sauntered into his house with two of her goons and taunted him about Laura's death. Enraged, Derek had attacked them. But Kate had laid him low with a cattle prod. She reminded him that there were bite marks on Laura's body. The Alpha had killed her, Kate insisted. So why didn't she and Derek help each other out? If Derek told her who the Alpha was, Kate could get rid of him for both Derek and the hunters.

But once she'd realized that Derek didn't know who the Alpha was, she'd decided he was expendable. That was why she'd tried to machine-gun him to death—and nearly brought down the house. His house and he were the last of the Hales—except for his uncle Peter Hale, a scarred vegetable wasting away at Beacons Crossing Home, a long-term-care facility. Derek could still remember Uncle Peter before the fire—a prankster with a wicked sense of humor.

Before the fire that the Argents set. I know they did it.

Derek did another set of push-ups. His back and chest were glistening with sweat and his arm muscles were aching. He ignored the pain and did another set of reps. He was driven. He needed endurance, and strength.

It was only a matter of time before Kate came back, and he had to be ready.

To tear her apart.

Meanwhile, he had other things on his mind. He'd had a dream, and he never dreamed. It hadn't been so much a dream as a nightmare, and it had awakened him at 3 a.m.— the hour of the wolf—when he bolted upright, sweating and panting, as if he'd been running for hours.

In his dream, he'd been trapped in the forest, and it had been burning all around him. And the only way out was blocked by the Alpha, whose gravelly voice carried over the firestorm: "It's almost time. My time. You follow me, or you die."

The nightmare Alpha showed itself then, massive, his eyes glowing scarlet, his mouth bristling with fangs. He rose on his hind legs, his howl victorious as he displayed dominance over the werewolf before him—Derek Hale, his inferior in status and strength.

In a heartbeat, Derek shifted. He attacked, taking the Alpha head-on, attempting to fling the huge monster onto his back. The Alpha swiped at Derek's head, but Derek flattened himself on the ground, rolling over. Assuming Derek was displaying submission,

*the Alpha lowered his massive paw as he stared Derek down. But
instead of averting his gaze to accept his junior rank, Derek bared
his teeth and went for the Alpha's throat.*

*The Alpha roared in fury at Derek's arrogance, rose on his hind
legs, and threw back his head, keeping his neck well out of Derek's
reach. Then his brought down his front leg again, this time slashing
Derek in the flank.*

I can't win this, *he thought, but his wolf brain said* Kill him.
Before he kills you. Because he will. He will come at you
and at you—

There will be many Alphas, other Alphas; each one you
kill will bring another. There will be blood on your hands
forever. This one, today; another one, tomorrow.

And on Wolf Moon . . . legions.

Humans will try to destroy you.

If they fail, an Alpha will succeed.

Derek had jerked awake in his sleeping bag with a growl.
Then, before he could forget, he strained to recall how the
voice of the Alpha had sounded. Male? Female? Maybe if
he could remember, he would have a clue as to the Alpha's
identity. The Alpha had bitten Scott McCall, and was urg-
ing Scott to kill with him. Once Scott did that—and he
would—the Alpha would own him. And it would be that
much harder for Derek to defeat the Alpha and avenge his
family.

There are a few people I'd like to kill, he thought, but no
way would he put himself under the control of an Alpha
he didn't even know. And besides, what he'd told Scott was
true: as a werewolf, he, Derek, might be a predator, but he
wasn't a killer. There was a difference, and anyone who'd

been born a werewolf and raised by werewolf parents would know that. Scott had simply been bitten, apparently at random, and if he, Derek, didn't teach him how to deal with it, Scott would wind up either under the control of the Alpha or dead.

Dead, because Derek would kill Scott himself, rather than allow him to expose the existence of werewolves to the humans who lived in Beacon Hills. Scott had threatened to tell Chris Argent everything. That was when Derek had taken Scott to see Uncle Peter, make him see that the Argents were ruthless killers. Eleven members of Derek's family had died in the fire that had swept through this house six years ago. Men, women, children. Not all of them werewolves.

And none of them deserving of the hideous, fiery death dealt to them by the Argents.

His sister, Laura, had been his Alpha after their family had been destroyed. And now she was dead. She'd been cut into pieces and left as bait to bring Derek back to Beacon Hills. Derek had assumed the Argents had killed her, but Kate had sworn they hadn't—just before she'd tried to cut Derek in half with a barrage of submachine-gun fire. Cold-hearted bitch. If ever someone *had* deserved to die . . .

Growling, he clenched his jaw against his fury, switching from two-armed push-ups to single-hand. He had to stay strong and fast. Or the next time the fire came, it might devour him, too.

Maybe that was what the dream had meant—he was going to be faced with a choice, and soon. He didn't like being squeezed between an unknown Alpha and the Argents. And having to deal with Scott on top of that. Derek needed a pack, others to make him stronger. And the only way that could happen was if he either joined the Alpha's pack as a Beta, or became an Alpha himself by killing the Alpha. Right now he was a lone wolf, and most lone wolves had short life spans.

But that wasn't the entire dream, he reminded himself. *I dreamed about other Alphas coming after me. Why? It's not a crime to kill an Alpha. I'm a werewolf. The way we progress in status is through challenge. If my opponent won't back down, it's within my rights to take what's mine in any way I can. Even death.*

Derek was deeply troubled. After the push-ups, he tore out of the house and jogged shirtless through the forest, aware of the scents of rabbits and squirrels, the rot of undergrowth, the piney scent of trees. He felt the blood pumping through his veins, the strength of his body, his endurance. As difficult as his life might have become, he wouldn't trade it for the relatively safer but dull, bland life as a human. He used to work off all the extra testosterone by swimming laps. That was how he had met *her*.

He raced up into the hills, gazing down at his home, and farther down, a few of the buildings of Beacon Hills. Then he caught the scent of a wolf—a full, natural wolf, not a werewolf. He sniffed again to make sure. What was it doing there? There hadn't been any natural wolves in California in more than sixty years.

Then he caught the scent of Scott McCall. Fresh. Recent. Scott had been in the forest this morning. Doing what?

Spying on me?

Derek let loose a low growl. He wanted to shift but he controlled himself. It was day, and you never knew who was watching.

Or plotting.

Like I am, he thought.

Scott rode shotgun in Allison's car, reading off the directions on his smartphone while Allison kept driving east, moving from the regular part of town to the bad part of town, and creeping ever closer into what was definitely the worst part of town. Scott had had no idea that such a place even existed. Allison's car glided past blocks of boarded-up buildings, liquor stores, pawnshops, and some kind of clinic where you could sell your blood.

"Remind me never to get a blood transfusion," he muttered. "The doors are locked, right?"

She toggled the power-lock button and gave him a quick nod.

"So you've never been to this neighborhood, either," Allison said. She looked cautiously through the windshield. "No wonder Lydia didn't want to come."

Scott frowned, seriously pissed off at Lydia for talking Allison into doing this. He was really glad he'd come with her.

She slowed as a guy in a filthy coat started pushing a shopping cart bulging with trash bags across the street. Scott cocked his head, listening. The man was rambling to himself, counting by twos.

"Don't stop. Just go around him," he cautioned.

She nodded and did as he asked. Scott couldn't imagine being in this neighborhood after nightfall. He wondered where the homeless man went to sleep. Scott definitely didn't picture him and Allison sleeping anywhere near here. So much for that dream.

We're kids anyway, he thought. *No one would rent a room to us. Well, except maybe around here.*

Allison glanced over at him. They had almost arrived at their location. He didn't want to think of Allison getting out of the car. They should turn around and get out of there.

"Allison, let's leave," he blurted.

She glanced over at him. "You're scared?"

"Yeah, aren't you?" he replied honestly.

She pressed her lips together and nodded. "This place is really terrible, Scott. I *want* to leave. But if Jackson's here, he might need help."

But not our help, he wanted to say. *Sheriff Stilinski's help, maybe.*

Almost as if she could read his mind, she said, "I promised Lydia I'd check the motel."

He heard the stubbornness in her tone of voice. It was obvious he wasn't going to be able to talk her out of going through with the plan. He thought about asking her to stay in the car, but the problem was, he didn't think she'd be any safer alone in the car than out on the street with him. Except, if he got too stressed and shifted, then she'd be in even greater danger.

I can't let it happen, he thought. *I won't.* He'd just have to keep reminding himself of that.

Allison's phone rang and Scott nearly jumped out of his skin. He looked at the caller ID.

"It's Lydia," he said.

"Put her on speaker," Allison asked him.

"Hi, have you found anything?" Lydia's voice was distorted. Allison's cell phone reception was weak. Another strike against going to the motel.

"Just three dozen strip clubs and a place to pawn my birthday necklace," Allison said a little heatedly. "Oh, look, there's another liquor store. With iron bars across the windows. Tell me the truth, Lydia. Did you *know* just how bad it is around here?"

"I thought it would be gross but . . . how bad?" Lydia asked, sounding contrite.

"Way bad," Allison said. "I'm kind of wishing I had pepper spray or something."

Me, too, Scott thought.

"I'm sorry I asked you to go," Lydia admitted. "I've never actually been to the bad part of town." She fell silent, as if she were trying to decide what to say next. Scott respected that silence. Lydia was clearly having a crisis of conscience. She wanted to find Jackson, but she didn't want to put Allison in harm's way. Scott liked her for that.

"Have you come up with anything?" Allison asked her.

"Well, I searched the Net for Hunter Gramm and nothing came up," Lydia replied.

"That's not good," Allison said, and Scott nodded, agreeing. "Maybe it's an alias, for when he goes undercover or something."

"Or it's a big scam. But Jackson never falls for things like that, and there've been a few people trying to shake money out of the Whittemores with all kinds of crazy schemes. Fake charities, supposed long-lost relatives. So he knows the drill. When you're part of a wealthy family, you get cynical."

So that's what it's called, Scott thought.

"So . . . this detective—not a detective?" Allison asked.

"I don't know. Jackson would be supercautious. He'd need proof." She sighed. "But he's been off his game lately. In more ways than one," she added languidly. "Maybe this has something to do with that."

"Well, we'll see what we can find out," Allison promised her.

Scott groaned inwardly. It was time for them to hang a left, but he didn't tell Allison. He wanted them to just leave. Jackson was so not worth it.

But Allison must have remembered his rundown of their route, because she put on her blinker and they turned the corner, facing a plain, two-story beige stucco building that said Thrifty Inn. It wasn't an inn by any stretch of the imagination, but it was at least five times nicer than Scott had anticipated, given what they'd driven through to get to it.

Allison looked over at Scott. "The motel's not that bad," she murmured. "We can just go in the lobby and ask. I have a picture of Jackson on my phone."

Why is that? Scott felt a little flare of jealousy, and he wanted to ask her about it. Then he calmed down a little, figuring Lydia had sent it to her specifically so they could show it to John Doe, Jane Smith, and Bambi von Boob Job.

"Okay," he said reluctantly.

"Okay, we're going . . ." Allison said, and then the phone dinged.

"Call failed," Scott reported, frowning down at her phone. He pulled out his own and checked his reception. Five bars, looking good.

"Well, I guess we were done talking," Allison said.

"Park there," Scott said, pointing to a streetlamp. Allison nodded and pulled to the curb. Scott cocked his head and willed his enhanced werewolf vision into action. He knew his eyes were glowing amber as he swept his gaze around, seeing everything in infrared, looking for details he would miss as a human. He climbed out first and scanned the area carefully. He saw nothing that threatened danger.

And he didn't sense the presence of the Alpha.

He walked over to the driver's side and gave Allison a nod. She pushed open the door and flashed him a quick, uncertain smile in return. "Opening my door is very chivalrous of you, Scott. But you know I'm not a girly girl."

"Me, neither," he said, "but the sooner we're out of here, the lower my voice will get."

She had the best dimples when she smiled. He took her hand and laced his fingers through hers, marveling at how soft her skin was. She smelled great—like flowers, maybe roses—and the sun caught gold strands in her dark chestnut hair. He felt a little wistful as they walked together to the front door of the motel. He sure didn't want his first time with Allison—his first time with *anybody*—to be in a place like this. But it was still only early afternoon, and she had a stay-out-of-jail-free card: her parents' permission not to be home until tomorrow. So maybe . . .

. . . somewhere else.

Beside the door, there was a sign beside a turquoise metal square with a white doorbell button that read Press for Entrance.

"Here goes nothing," he said, raising his hand.

Just as Scott pushed the button, a woman started screaming.

CHAPTER FOUR

Kate Argent sighted down the brand-new Uzi submachine gun as her brother Chris and the other hunters
unloaded the fresh cache of weapons from the black panel
van and stored them in the Argents' garage. The Uzi was a
little piece of heaven. Nothing beat the feel of cold, hard
steel—unless it was the rippling muscles of a well-built man.

Smirking, she thought of Derek's naked torso, how well
he filled out his jeans. His piercing eyes, those eyebrows she
used to trace so fondly; and that five o'clock shadow and
sexy bad-boy pout. She highly doubted that Chris knew she
and two of his guys had paid Derek a little visit yesterday.
God, all those muscles. The last time she'd seen him, he'd
still been in high school. Still a kid. A stupid, gullible kid,
who should have died in the Hale house fire along with the
rest of his family.

Talk about your loose end.

She pulled the trigger at a nonexistent target, imagining a werewolf kill with the unloaded weapon. Maybe she
should have taken advantage of Derek while he'd been

down on the floor, writhing from the nine hundred thousand volts she'd sent skittering through his kick-ass body. For old time's sake.

Kate was all about taking advantage.

"I have egg salad and cold cuts," Chris's wife, Victoria, announced as she brought out a tray of sandwiches from the house. Victoria was wearing jeans and a short-sleeved black turtleneck sweater with a lot of gold chains. Her pixie haircut set off her big blue eyes.

Kate highly approved of her sister-in-law's efforts to keep the troops well fed. What was the saying? An army traveled on its stomach? It sounded gross, but it was true. And while you couldn't say they were an army, exactly, they definitely needed to keep up their strength. There was an Alpha in town, and two Betas, and in some ways, werewolves were like the bunnies they were so fond of ripping to pieces: they tended to multiply.

And they tended to love sex. At least, Derek did.

She sighed and put down the Uzi. Then she joined her brother as he examined a carton containing a bunch of Glock pistols. Ulrich, one of the guys who'd gone out hunting with her at Derek's house, gave Kate a secretive nod as he stored a box of ammo inside a cabinet. His face was a little bruised from when Derek had thrown him across the room. What had he expected, with his stupid joke about Derek burying a bone in the yard?

Of course, he had, hadn't he? His sister's bones.

The call on Derek had been a rough morning for Kate's two henchmen, but it had also been fruitful, if in a dead-end sort of way. It was obvious to Kate that Derek didn't know who the Alpha was, and her first impulse was to kill him, because he was therefore useless. But she was actually glad she'd failed. Because he was still very useful. Maybe they could flush out the Alpha by observing him. If only she could figure out who the second Beta was. Maybe the sheriff's kid. Maybe the one with the werewolf claw marks on his neck. What was his name—Jackson?

"Kate," her brother said, and she shook herself out of her reverie. "I asked you if you're weapons-qualified on these." He picked up one of the Glocks and held it out to her.

"Oh, yeah, I am," she cooed, wrapping her hand lovingly around the handle. "You have to watch for the slight recoil. But if you're prepared, this is a really sweet weapon." She smiled at him. "Like me."

His gray eyes were hooded as he studied her. "You've had a busy year."

"You know it, big brother. But you know I'm never too busy for you."

"*You* called *me*, remember?" he said.

"As soon as I heard," she replied. She flashed a sly grin at a hot Scandinavian type—total Thor material—walking behind her brother with a sandwich in one hand and a beer in the other. She'd like to chew that one up and swallow him whole.

"I'm going to get him for you, Chris," she told her brother. "That Alpha and his two Betas. For your birthday." She trailed her fingers along the gun, then set it back down.

"We do it by the code, Kate," Chris said, somber, stern. "Just like we always have."

"Right. By the code." She looked at the weapons cabinet, already bulging with firepower. "What are you going to tell Allison about all these new weapons? That you made a great sale to the Beacon Hills Sheriff's Department and they're going to take over California?"

"Allison's a good girl," he said automatically, and then a cloud passed over his face.

Kate silently chuckled. Daddy's good girl had just cut her first day of school, and Chris had laid down the law—for about twelve hours. It was Allison's unbelievable good fortune that this weapons cache had arrived today. Chris was uneasy about how close Allison was getting to the truth about her family, so he had given her permission to "go study" at some girl's house.

Yeah, right. Kate would bet her soul that Allison was with some *boy*. That cute guy, Scott, with the adorable brown eyes, to be specific. Warming the bench while he played lacrosse, with plans to warm him later. That little scamp had tried to snitch a condom out of Kate's luggage.

Protection is good, Kate thought. That was why she'd given Allison the necklace with the Beast on it. The Argents were surrounded by enemies, and the sooner Allison knew that, the better. Chris was crippling his daughter by keeping all their secrets . . . secret. What was going to happen when the *really* big guns showed up?

Allison was the new generation of a centuries-old family of hunters. *The* family. And they were locked in a war that wouldn't be over until the last werewolf was dead—at least, as far as Kate was concerned. The code—*We hunt those who hunt us*—was an outmoded relic of a different time. It had never worked—look at their history. It sure as hell wasn't going to start working anytime soon. Not now, and not here.

Protection is vital.

"You didn't used to care if Allison was home when you got a delivery," Kate said, pushing him a little. "She knows you sell weapons, so what's the big deal?"

He didn't answer, but he got a funny look on his face, and Kate was intrigued. Maybe there was some kind of new weapon in these boxes. Something designed specifically to take out werewolves. She had her trusty bullets loaded with Northern Blue Monkshood, but she was always up for something new and different. Especially if it delivered an agonizing, painful death.

I thought I'd shot that Beta when I came into town, she mused. *If I had, it would be dead. Maybe what I hit was just a big old cat. Poor kitty.*

"Kate? Sandwich?" Victoria invited her, holding out the tray.

Kate grinned and took two sandwiches, one for each hand. "I'm starving," she declared.

The woman screamed just as the buzzer on the motel's front door went off. Scott's first instinct was to throw his arms around Allison and duck, but she yanked open the door and barreled inside the motel like a superhero. He had no option but to trail after her.

"Allison, wait!" he yelled.

They entered a tiny, dingy room with nothing in it but a

dusty counter littered with papers and a cash register. Behind the counter there was a closed door with a sign on it that read Pay in Advance—Cash Only. And to the left of the counter, a curtain made of strands of wooden beads swayed in an open doorway, signaling that someone had passed through.

They heard another scream, high-pitched and frightened. Scott pulled out his phone to call 911, but Allison ran through the beads and he had no choice but to go in after her.

"No!" he called. "Allison!"

Then she seemed to realize what she was doing. She turned on her heel and looked at him, just as the door to her left crashed open and a woman wearing a short shiny black bathrobe and a man in a pair of jeans and a sleeveless T-shirt almost crashed into her. The woman's hair was bleached white-blond and her eyes were rimmed with heavy black liner.

"He said he saw something at the window!" the woman shouted.

Other doors were opening, and heads were peering around them, revealing unshaven men, and women who had seen better days.

At least, Scott hoped they had.

"I called 911," the woman said. She looked around at the open doors. "Anyone here know CPR?"

"Who's hurt?" Allison asked.

"No one's *hurt*," the man said. He shook his head at the blonde. "Tawny, the guy in your room is *dead*."

"No, he can't be. Oh, poor, poor . . . man," the woman—Tawny—said, dissolving into tears. "Poor . . . whoever."

Scott realized Tawny didn't even know the dead man's name.

"He said he was going to take care of me, get me my own place. And now he's *dead*? And I didn't even get paid!" She started to go back into the room. "Just let me get what I'm owed." Her sorrow had dried up along with her tears. Now she was all business.

The man grabbed her arm. "I've got that handled," he murmured. "Come with me."

They started to walk past Scott and Allison. Then the man halted. "You need a room?" he asked Scott.

"No," Scott said, stunned by his callousness. Then he recovered and said, "But we're looking for somebody. "A guy."

"This guy," Allison said, clearing her throat as she held up her phone. Jackson was wearing his lacrosse uniform with his helmet against his hip.

"Never seen him," the man said.

"What happened to the man in there?" Scott looked at the woman. "You said he saw something in the window?"

"Yeah, he was going to smoke a cigarette. And Charlie"—she gestured to the man—"doesn't like the customers . . . er, *guests*, to smoke in their rooms, so he was going to open the window. So my, um, friend goes to the window and he pulls open the curtain and he shouts, 'What the hell!' and then he grabs his chest and he falls down." She shuddered. "And I guess he died then."

"What did he see?" Scott asked. It had to have been something terrifying. Sheriff Stilinski had some really blurry pictures of the Alpha crashing through the window at the video store. He couldn't figure out what he was looking at.

But maybe the guy who died saw the Alpha face-to-face, staring at him through his window.

"I don't know, but it scared him bad," she said. "I've never had anyone die on me before. Except for the other time."

Scott detected the whine of a siren. He was about to say something when he realized no one else had heard it yet. If it was Stiles's dad, Scott totally did not want to explain what he was doing with Allison Argent in a place like this.

Meanwhile, some of the other "guests" had shut their doors. Scott couldn't imagine being so hard-hearted that you could go back to whatever you were doing after someone had just died. The deaths that the "mountain lion" had caused had upset everyone Scott knew.

"Hey, excuse me. Have you seen this guy?" Allison asked a woman who was still watching from her doorway.

But the woman hadn't seen Jackson, and the siren had grown loud enough that Allison could hear it. She looked anxiously at Scott, who said, "We'd better go," and she nodded.

They headed back through the reception area, to see the man in the T-shirt and the woman who'd been crying counting out dollar bills together. Scott realized that they'd taken the cash from the dead man. The woman flushed and the man avoided Scott's gaze as Scott opened the door and together he and Allison hurried to her car. She was about to turn on the engine when the sheriff's white car, followed by an ambulance, screeched up to the curb just in front of them. In unison, Scott and Allison scooted down in their seats to hide.

Peering up through the side window, Scott watched as Stiles's father strode into the motel, followed by two guys from the ambulance in navy blue jumpsuits pushing a gurney. The clatter of the gurney's wheels ricocheted inside Scott's head like a pinball game.

He grimaced, hoping the guy in the T-shirt and the blonde didn't mention two kids looking for a third.

"Okay, so this was . . . horrible," Allison murmured. They stayed scooched down in their seats, and Scott counted off a couple of minutes. "Do you think it's safe to leave yet?"

As if on cue, he heard the clattering wheels again. The door to the motel opened, and one of the paramedics pushed out the gurney. A heavyset, balding man lay beneath a blanket that was pulled up to his shoulders. A mask covered most of his face, and it was attached to what Scott guessed was a canister of oxygen. The second paramedic was holding on to the canister and squeezing it while jogging alongside.

"Oh, look, he's alive," Allison said happily.

I should find out what he saw in the window, Scott thought. *Why would the Alpha be around here?*

Faintly, Scott could hear Stiles's dad questioning the man in the T-shirt, who was Charlie, the manager. Scott focused hard.

"*Older guys, you know how it is, when they're, y'know, having a good time. The ol' ticker speeds up, they have a heart attack. It wasn't nothing else.*"

"*Yeah,*" Stiles's dad said. "*Well, thanks for your help.*"

"*I run a clean place,*" Charlie went on. "*Nothing going on here that shouldn't be.*"

"I think we should go now," Scott said.

Allison started the car and shot away from the curb. Scott craned his neck to look back at the motel, allowing his enhanced vision to take over—risky, he knew, with Allison right beside him. He couldn't let her see his glowing eyes. He counted off a row of windows, which were almost entirely hidden from his view by a row of dark green bushes. It would be simple for something to creep along those bushes and peek in. There might be footprints—paw prints—beneath the window.

He wanted to follow the ambulance to the hospital, but he wasn't sure he should do it around Allison. What if the guy said something incriminating? *I saw a monster?* So what if he did? Allison would have no reason to believe him—or to connect that to Scott.

Allison's phone trilled, signaling a text. He hesitated, torn between reading the message and respecting her privacy.

"Is that Lydia?" she asked.

He looked. *Call me ASAP,* the text said. *L.*

"She wants you to call her," he affirmed.

"She's on speed dial," she said. "Press two."

Scott wondered if he rated being on her speed dial. He didn't ask, just called Lydia, who answered on the first ring. He put her on speaker.

"What have you two been doing?" Lydia cried. "You were supposed to call me back right away!"

"This man had a heart attack," Allison said, her voice shrill. "He said he saw something in a window. They thought he was dead."

"A . . . window?" Lydia sounded odd.

"Yes," Allison said, trading looks with Scott. He shrugged.

"But he wasn't dead?" Lydia said.

"No."

"Were you able to ask about Jackson?"

"No one saw him," Allison said.

"Well, now he's in the Beacon Hills Preserve," Lydia said. "I refreshed the search. That's why I asked you to contact me."

"The forest? What's he doing there?" Allison asked. "Did he call you?"

"No," Lydia said, her voice low and tense. "I should probably go with you this time."

Go with us? We are going? Scott thought, alarmed. He gave a quick shake of his head. He didn't want Allison anywhere near the woods today. Not after his dream, and the window, and Jackson still missing.

"No, that's okay," Allison said, nodding at him to show that she understood what he was trying to say. "We're closer. If we have to double back to pick you up, we'll lose time. There's only so much daylight."

That's not what I was going for, Scott thought. She had completely misread his head shake.

"Allison, that's really sweet, but Jackson's my boyfriend. My responsibility," Lydia said.

"But what if my parents call your house?" Allison said. "We're supposed to be showing up there soon, after 'the library.' You need to be there to intercept their calls."

"Wow, I'm impressed," Lydia drawled. "You definitely have a future as a party girl. God knows why your parents would bother mine, but we do still have a landline. It'll be no problem to patch you in as a conference call and tell them you're on an extension. But to do all that, I *do* to need to be here."

"Right," Allison said. "It'll work as long as I have good cell phone reception."

Scott stared at her, torn between being impressed, like Lydia, and worried that he was being a bad influence. He'd never figured Allison for a techie—or someone who would sneak around like that. Him and Stiles, yeah, but they had good reason.

Well, I'm her *good reason,* he thought, smiling faintly at Allison.

"I'm e-mailing you the page with the Where's My Phone map," Lydia said. "That'll help you find him faster."

"Okay. Send the WMP map to Scott's, too."

The two hung up and Scott turned to Allison. "Whoa," he said. "An A in butt covering."

She flushed. "I know what you're thinking, and no, I have *never* snuck around behind my parents' backs before. All that call-forwarding stuff actually came up in a class discussion back in San Francisco about government surveillance."

He held up his hands. "It's cool. But maybe you should go back to Lydia's," he said. "If your parents find out you're with me, they'll totally freak."

"They won't find out." But the look on her face revealed her concern. "Look, we know where Jackson is, and we're pretty close to the preserve. Let's just go check it out."

He frowned. "It's not a good idea."

She hesitated. "Scott, what? Are you scared? My dad killed the mountain lion. Things are back to normal."

That sounded so odd, coming from her. Things had not been "normal" since she'd moved there. But as far as he could tell, she didn't know that her father was a hunter, and she for sure didn't know that she was dating one of the hunted.

"It'll be okay," she told him. "It's still light out. We'll only stay as long as the sun's up."

He was mortified. She was trying to talk him into going because she thought he was a big chicken. He rolled down the window and mimicked dropping something out of the car.

"Did you just throw something out the window?" she asked him as she stopped at a red light.

"Yeah. My masculinity." He quirked a smile. "I just didn't want *you* to go into the woods, Allison. I mean, what if you get hurt or something? Your parents will find out and—"

She brushed her lips against his. "I can take care of myself," she murmured.

No, you really can't, he thought, but he knew that was the last thing he should say to her. Along with the rush of her kiss, a wave of protectiveness washed over him. Maybe it was habit. He looked out for his mom, who was struggling to keep everything going—pay the bills, keep the car going, stop the roof falling in. And now he looked out for Allison, too. The women he . . . loved.

I just said I loved her. To myself, yeah, but still, I said it. He

felt . . . different. Happy. Maybe a little scared. And like he'd
just found out something very important that would change
his life as much as becoming a werewolf had changed it.

He felt both as if he had more power, and less.

Floating, and falling.

"Okay," he said. "Let's go."

CHAPTER FIVE

I didn't know there was a road here," Scott said as he and Allison wound through woods so dense the sun was all but blotted out. He carefully turned his head away from her and searched the shadows with his werewolf vision, watching a deer back away and turn tail as the car approached. Birds scattered from the trees. He thought of the cats in the vet clinic, how they had yowled and hissed the afternoon after he'd been bitten. They knew the wolf lurked inside him. It was probably a good thing his mom had given up on having pets because of his asthma. How would he have explained his own cat or dog flipping out every time he came into a room?

Allison cast him a sidelong glance, as if she still thought he was afraid to go this far into the preserve. Mostly, he was trying to figure out if the road could serve as a shortcut to the Hale house. He wanted to keep Derek as far away from Allison as possible.

Then they reached a length of chain strung across the road. A No Trespassing sign dangled from the middle. Scott wondered if it marked the beginning of Hale land. He didn't really know very much about the Hales. He dimly remembered hearing about the fire. He would have been ten years old when it had happened.

He checked the map on his phone. Jackson—or his phone—was located well past the chain. Allison leaned over and studied it, too; then she looked from the chain to the woods and back again.

"I guess we go on foot from here," she said. "Let me check in again with Lydia first."

He approved of her caution, and texted Stiles while he waited.

Guy at motel had heart attack. Think he saw. Go to hospital and try to find out, kk?

Saw what? Stiles texted back.

Think u know, Scott replied. He could tell by Allison's conversation that Lydia still hadn't heard from Jackson, and she was getting pretty worried. Allison was trying to comfort her by reminding her, *"You know how guys are,"* and Scott was insulted. Maybe some guys would go all silent like Jackson had, but he would never worry Allison like that.

I'd just lie to her about where I'd been, like I've been doing ever since I met her.

Except . . . he had never lied, exactly. Not yet, anyway.

Allison hung up. She had the world's longest eyelashes. There was real worry in those dark brown eyes.

"I just don't get why he hasn't checked in with her, if he's okay," she said.

"Because he's Jackson?" Scott blurted, then glanced down at his phone as it dinged, indicating the arrival of a message.

Got motel guy's name off Dad's police scanner. Alan Seber. Going to hospital.

KK, thanks, Scott texted back.

"You'd just think he'd let her know," Allison said. She reached behind to the passenger seat and grabbed a warm coat. The gray one. Scott had on a sweatshirt, but he didn't really need it. The cold didn't bother him anymore. That wasn't a big enough plus to make him glad he'd been bitten, unlike what Derek had promised. He'd claimed Scott would grow to love being a werewolf. So far?

No love to be had.

Either Danny had been taking advanced goalie lessons, or he had had a side dish of irritation along with his Gatorade because Jackson hadn't told him where he was. Either way, he exceeded his four seconds. Then they ran out of hot water in the showers and by then, Stiles had been very happy to be in his room, at home, checking up on the ever-growing mob of zombie sheep in his MMORPG. He kept one ear open for good stuff on his dad's police scanner.

Then Scott e-mailed him a map featuring a very narrow, one-lane road leading into Beacon Hills Preserve. It looked like you could use it as a back way to get to the preserve from the Hale house.

Chalk one up for technology.

And one for the Hales.

He read Scott's text about the heart attack. " 'Saw,' " he murmured. He listened to the scanner and got the motel guy's name. He texted back, muttering, "So, Scott, saw what? Saw Derek?"

"Yes?" Derek said from behind him.

"Yeaooww!" Stiles shouted. He turned around to find Derek leaning against the wall. He did that on an irritatingly frequent basis, both at Scott's house and Casa Stilinksi. He was wearing his black leather jacket and he looked especially pouty and broody. "Could you not do that anymore? It is so not cool."

Derek leaned over Stiles's shoulder and picked up his phone. "What motel guy? What's Scott doing? Where is he?"

"Doin' stuff," Stiles said.

Derek looked disgusted and held out Stiles's phone to him. "Tell him to meet me."

"He's kinda busy," Stiles said.

"Stiles?" Stiles jerked at the sound of his father's voice from the hallway.

"Gotta get that." Stiles pointedly shut down his desktop—Derek actually growled—and slid his phone into the pocket of his jeans. "Don't touch anything," he ordered the werewolf.

Then he left his room, shutting the door, and went to see what his father wanted. His dad was leaning against the kitchen counter drinking a glass of milk.

"How was lacrosse practice?" he asked.

"Fine," Stiles said. He waited for his dad to get to the point.

"Good." He paused with his glass against his chest. "What's your homework like for the weekend?"

"It's there," Stiles said, then realized this conversation

was fallout from the very suckish parent-teacher conference. Then he threw caution to the winds and said, "Okay, I
admit it, I was listening to the scanner. Some guy at a motel
had a heart attack?"

His father narrowed his eyes. "Stiles, how many
times . . ." he began, then nodded. "Yes."

"Just . . . keeled over?"

His dad finished his glass of milk, rinsed it out, and put
it into the dish drainer. For some reason, that made Stiles
think of his mother, and that made him miss her a little
more than usual. Life in his head was accompanied by the
soundtrack of a small, eternal, dull ache, but word was that
would go away after a few decades.

"Why do you care about some guy in a motel?" his dad
asked him.

"I care about all mankind, Dad," Stiles said, and his father
gave him an eye roll.

"Where's your partner in crime?"

"Home, I guess." Stiles concentrated on the big-eyed-
puppy-dog look. It was clear his dad wasn't buying, and
Stiles wanted to go back to his room to make sure Derek
wasn't, um, *sniffing* around. "But I'll get right on all that
homework," he said. He turned to go, turned back. "So the
motel guy, is he going to be okay?"

"I'd suspect you of something, if I could figure out what
it was," his father replied. "The motel guy is no longer my
responsibility. My field is criminal justice, not medicine." He
crossed to the kitchen table and picked up his olive green
lawman jacket. "I'm going back out."

"Did you get another call?" Stiles asked. "Is something going down?"

"Besides your grades?" His father cocked his head. "Did you take your Adderall today?"

"A gallon of it. Er, I mean, yes." Stiles gave him a salute. "I'll be in my room." Then, just in case, he added, "I'm probably getting together with Scott in a bit. His grades are even worse than mine. I want to help."

"You're quite the humanitarian."

Oh, yeah, right there was the proof that Stiles had definitely inherited his dry wit from his old man.

"You wound me, Dad," he said.

He zoomed back into his room to find Derek clacking away on his computer keyboard. It seemed so bizarre that an actual werewolf was sitting at his desk, but not as bizarre that his best friend had been turned into a werewolf.

"Hey," he said. "Keep your paws off." Derek gave him one of his trademark sour glares and Stiles said, "The deal with the motel guy is that he saw something at a window and it freaked him out so badly he had a heart attack. It wasn't you, was it?"

"No," Derek said, but he looked interested.

"Okay, well, I'm going to the hospital to see if he'll tell me what it was."

Derek looked uncomfortable. There was something up about him and the hospital. Maybe the fact that half of his sister had wound up in the morgue had put him off the place. Stiles doubted it was the cafeteria food.

"Why would he tell you?" Derek asked.

"Or . . . maybe the nurses will gossip," Stiles said.

"I'll go with you," Derek announced.

"Na-uh," Stiles protested. He'd just had his daily quota of five minutes with Derek and he certainly didn't want to overdo it. "You won't."

"Look." Derek leaned toward him and the hairs on the back of Stiles's neck stood straight up. "You and I both know that guy might have seen the Alpha. And if I can find the Alpha, I can help Scott. So I'm going with you."

"Okay, okay," Stiles said. "You can follow in your car."

"I didn't come here in a car," Derek said.

"Okay, fine," Stiles said, displeased. Maybe if Derek *did* drive his car more often, instead of jogging all over the place like the Flash, he could cut down on the risk that someone might start to wonder about That Guy with the Eyebrows. He'd already been arrested for murder once—for the death of his sister, actually. Stiles and Scott had had a little something to do with that. Okay, a lot, by announcing that they had found Laura Hale's torso buried beside Derek's house. But Sheriff Dad's crack forensics team had found wolf hairs, and not human hairs, on Laura Hale's corpse. So Derek had been set free.

"But don't do anything wolfy in my Jeep," he said, opening up his door and peering into the hallway. The coast was clear. "Like stick your head out the window and let your tongue hang out—"

"Shut up," Derek said. "Let's go."

•   •   •

What was that?

As surreptitiously as he could, Scott cocked his head and listened to the faint echo of the cracking of a twig. Oblivious, Allison was picking her way down an incline. She had swapped out her heeled boots for flat ones better suited for hiking. It was too bad that she kept so much stuff in her trunk—he could have used the excuse that she wasn't dressed for investigating the preserve to avoid bringing her there.

Another twig cracked. Allison didn't hear that one, either. When she caught him looking at her, she gave her hair a toss beneath her knitted cap and kissed his cheek. His anxious frown melted into a grin. Her kiss had made his heart skip a beat.

"We should be close," she said, wrapping her hand around his and pulling the phone close so she could study the map. "Um, right?"

"It looks like it." He eased both their hands toward his chest, pulling her close, snagging another kiss. This one lasted longer. Then he put his free hand around her waist and held her as he kissed her again, slowly, savoring it. He felt as though the top of his head would explode. Allison was the first girl he had ever kissed—*really* kissed, not like in some dumb game like Truth or Dare. His heart thundered and he tried to remind himself that he couldn't get carried away. If he did, he might shift. And if he shifted . . .

"What was that?" she said, breaking the kiss.

That time, he had heard nothing but the roaring of his own pulse and the quickening of her heartbeat. Even now, he fought to concentrate, and to hear what had startled her.

Then, deep within his mind, he heard the howl of a wolf. It was like an echo inside an echo, and although it was faint, he heard it distinctly: one wolf calling another. Seeking the pack.

He blinked and slid a glance toward Allison, to see if she had heard it, too. She'd heard *something*.

"What?" he asked.

She frowned slightly, listening. Then she relaxed. "It was nothing. I guess," she added tentatively. "I thought I heard voices."

"Like Jackson?" He started to call out Jackson's name, then wondered if he should. There were two strikes against it: one was that if someone was in the woods who should not be—the Alpha—Scott didn't want to signal where he was. And the second was, well, it was pretty nice to be alone with Allison when she had her arms around him.

"Jackson?" she called, settling his debate by taking the choice away from him. "Are you here?"

They both listened for a moment. He didn't hear anything. No Jackson, no wolf howl. Maybe he had imagined it. He was still getting used to being a werewolf; it was hard to know what was really happening and what was going on, because he was changing, becoming something he'd never dreamed existed.

A breeze tickled Allison's hair against her cheeks as she stood poised, listening. He couldn't get over how beautiful she was. How warm her skin was, and how good she smelled.

"I guess not," she said. She pressed her body against his. "Now, where were we?"

Looking for Jackson, he almost replied. But that wasn't where they were. As he kissed her again, Jackson was far away from where they were.

On another planet, even.

Jackson had never spent much time in the Beacon Hills Preserve. He was either on the field, or in the gym lifting weights, or with Lydia. He didn't know his way around and he didn't appreciate coating his Porsche's custom rims with mud. But now he was standing in front of a crackling campfire, exactly where Hunter Gramm had instructed him to meet, and if the guy didn't show within the next thirty seconds, Jackson was done.

"I don't appreciate being jerked around," he called into the darkness.

"I'm here," a voice called out. Its owner sounded surprisingly young, maybe still in his twenties, and he was standing behind the fire in the shadows. Squinting, all Jackson could make out was his silhouette, painted up to his shins with orange flames. He was tall, and trim, and that was all Jackson could tell.

"I waited for you all night at that disgusting motel. Why didn't you show?" Jackson said.

"I got held up. I couldn't make it," Gramm replied.

"That's not good enough."

"And yet, it'll have to do."

Though tired, Jackson forced himself to stay alert and not get intimidated. Everything about this guy was wrong, and he'd been an idiot to take a chance like this. But things were so messed up. It was Scott McCall's fault. The little twerp had turned into Superman on the lacrosse field, executing all kinds of close-to-impossible gymnastics to steal the ball and racing down the field so fast he *had* to be on something. Jackson had called him on it, and next thing he knew, McCall's creepy drug dealer had shown up at school. When Jackson had stood up to him, he'd grabbed him by the neck and, like, *gouged* him with his fingernails.

The cuts McCall's supplier had left on the back of his neck weren't healing. And Jackson was having bad dreams. Terrible dreams. Okay, nightmares, all twisted and confused, like the ones drug addicts and little kids had. He didn't know how to explain what was happening to him. He was Jackson Whittemore, captain of the best lacrosse high school team in the state. Number one. He drove a frickin' Porsche. He had a hot girlfriend. Every guy at school wanted to be him.

Except . . . who was he?

"Well?" Jackson said, and his voice wobbled a little. He hated that wobble, hated betraying any sign that he was not in complete charge of the situation. Things had been fine before the start of the school year. Then it was almost as if McCall had concocted some kind of scheme over the summer to ruin his life.

"Well, we're here now, together, just the two of us," the guy in the shadows said. He called himself Hunter Gramm, but Jackson doubted that was his real name. "Right? Because what I have to tell you is just for you. No one else."

"Fine," Jackson said.

"And . . . you didn't tell anyone you were meeting me?" Gramm queried.

Jackson wasn't an idiot. You didn't go assuring complete strangers—potentially dangerous strangers—that you didn't have backup. But on the other hand, this guy had already told him that if he, Jackson, shared the contents of that note with anybody, the deal was off. There would be no information, no shared secrets from the lips of Hunter Gramm.

"Tell me what you have to tell me *now.*" Jackson glared at the shadowed outline. It was scaring him that Gramm wouldn't show his face. It was too much like his dreams of late. "Or I'm leaving."

"You sound so much like your father," Gramm said. He paused a beat and then added, "Your real father."

"My father is my real father," Jackson said tiredly. That was what his parents had drilled into him ever since the day they had told him he was adopted. *We are your real parents. We're not your birth parents, but we'll always be here for you.*

"Biological father, then," Gramm said. "The man in the picture I enclosed with my note."

Jackson had found the note crammed into his locker, and at first he'd thought it was some kind of joke. But a few hints tossed around among his friends had put that to rest. The picture was a tiny square, and it lay in the pocket of the jacket Jackson was wearing. In it, a guy was holding a newborn and smiling. And the guy looked just like Jackson, only a few years older. But not many. Jackson had studied that picture for hours in the motel, spinning a scenario that his parents had met in college; his mom had gotten pregnant, and they'd decided they were too young to raise a baby—

So they gave me up.

After all these years, that shouldn't hurt, but it did. His mom had gone on and on about all the advantages she and Dad had been able to offer him that two poor, scared kids could never have. But what he heard under her chatter was, *We love you, and they didn't.*

"So how did you know him?" Jackson demanded.

"*Do* I know him. My dad knows him," Gramm said. "But they don't know about you. I put it all together myself. I was reading about the up-and-coming lacrosse players, and I saw your picture. You look exactly like your father."

Jackson's mind reeled. *He's alive? He's around? Did he live nearby?*

"Prove it," Jackson flung at him, trying to regain the upper hand. But he was thrown. He thought he had psyched himself up for this meeting, but until now, the claims of the "private detective" had been hypothetical.

"He was talking about this kid he gave up. He said he liked to call you Q.B. For 'Quarterback.' He had those daddy dreams about raising an athletic kid. He'd be proud of you."

Jackson clenched his fists inside his pockets, careful not to bend the photo. "Q.B." sounded . . . right. It was almost familiar, a whisper against his memory, like when you couldn't bring to mind the name of a player on an opposing team but you knew that it would eventually come to you.

But his mom and dad had said they'd adopted him as an infant right out of the hospital. He couldn't remember something that hadn't happened.

Maybe my parents knew my father, he thought. He'd never

asked questions. But then, they'd never offered answers. It had been a "closed" adoption, they'd said. Meaning that the birth parents hadn't wanted to be contacted, ever. But was that true?

"So you lied about being a detective," Jackson said angrily.

"No, I didn't," Gramm replied. "I really am a private detective. Got a license and a job."

"You could have Photoshopped this picture and you *know* I'm in sports." He felt so stupid, and so disappointed. Before the start of the school year, and Scott McCall's crap? He wouldn't have thought about that note twice.

"You don't have the money to pay for my information," Gramm said. "Do you." It was not a question.

"Don't worry about getting paid," Jackson said, sneering at him. Everyone wanted something Jackson had. It was usually money or popularity. The secret? They were exactly the same thing.

"I'd feel better if you could give me a little sample of that money," Gramm pressed. Then he tossed something into the fire. Jackson pushed on the balls of his feet, ready to retrieve it, but it was just a scattering of leaves.

"I need proof that you've got something to sell," Jackson said.

"Oh, I do, Jackson. Address. Phone. All of it."

Jackson felt unsteady on his feet. If he could contact his father, would he? Was his mom still with him? He had a hundred questions, a million. If Hunter Gramm had answers, he'd get his money.

In the distance, there was a noise like the cracking of a twig. Gramm shifted his weight.

"I thought I told you to come alone," he said.

"We're in a forest," Jackson shot back, his way of replying without really answering. All kinds of things lived in the forest.

Then suddenly he felt the absolute certainty that they were being watched. And by the way the hair rose on the back of his neck, he was equally certain that he should get the hell out of there.

CHAPTER SIX

Oh my God, Scott thought, deliriously happy. *Allison is going to kiss me all night.*

She had her arms twined around him and they were making out like crazy. He kept pressing his forefinger and thumb together to check his nails—no wolfiness so far—so he kept going for it. He kept telling himself that in a couple of more seconds—or minutes—or maybe hours—he would suggest they go back to the car. There were a lot more things they could do in a car. But they could also *leave* in a car, and he was afraid he'd break the spell if he said a word.

And her kisses were so awesome. For someone who had never had a boyfriend before, she sure knew how to kiss.

She broke contact—*no*, he silently protested—and smiled at him. Then her eyes went wide as she gazed somewhere past him. He felt her stiffen.

"Scott," she whispered. "Behind you."

He cursed himself for being six kinds of stupid, taking a risk like this. In the instant before he turned around he realized that the sun was going down; the shadows of the trees had lengthened and darkness brought with it a lot of secrets, and more danger.

He tried to sniff the air as he pivoted around, preparing himself for action against whatever threat presented itself. And what he smelled was an animal.

A . . . wolf.

It was the same one that he had faced that morning. It was beautiful, standing slightly above them on a boulder. As with their dawn encounter, the wolf was bathed in light, the silver gray hair catching the slanting afternoon sun. It gazed at the two of them calmly, with no hint of aggression.

"Oh," Allison whispered. "It's . . . beautiful."

"It's a wild animal," Scott said in a low voice. "Don't move."

She nodded breathlessly. He tested his fingernails again. His wolf was staying inside.

So far.

"Can you get to your phone?" he asked her quietly. His first instinct was for her to summon help. Dial 911. But what could anyone do if the wolf attacked right this second? They had hiked in at least a mile, deep into the tangled trees of the preserve, where no emergency vehicles could possibly reach.

The wolf tilted its head and gazed at each of them in turn, Allison first. It locked gazes with Scott, holding, as if trying to tell him something. Allison's fingers tightened around Scott's. He squeezed back.

Then, just as it had done that morning, the wolf turned its back and ambled down the boulder. It disappeared among the trees. As if by mutual agreement, Scott and Allison didn't move a muscle. Scott could barely breathe.

After a minute or two, Allison relaxed. She wrapped both her hands around one of Scott's.

"That was . . ." she began.

"Intense," he finished.

"I've never seen anything more amazing in my life." She blew out a breath and looked at him, almost as if she'd never seen him before. "I can't believe I got to experience that."

"Got to . . ." He trailed off, surprised by her choice of words. His legs were rubbery. What would he have done if the wolf had attacked Allison?

I didn't think it would attack me, he realized. *I think it knew. Knew what I am.*

She leaned her head on his shoulder. "When my dad shot the mountain lion, I told myself I should be happy about it. I mean, it had killed all those people. But it was"— she looked for words—"innocent. In its way. I mean, here we are, in their territory. And we build our houses, and drive our cars."

She moved her shoulders, a little embarrassed. "Right about now, my aunt would ask me if I am planning to give PETA a donation. I mean, we sell *hunting* rifles, too. We're not what you might call tree huggers."

Scott moved her hair away from her forehead. "The wolf," he said. "You, you thought it was . . . beautiful?"

She nodded. "All that hair, or fur, or whatever you call it. And those sleek muscles underneath its pelt. Did you see its eyes, Scott? It looked . . . wise." She made a face. "Okay, now I'm romanticizing it. Let's say it was really cool to see a wild animal up close like that, and leave it at that."

She couldn't know how much her reaction meant to

him. Derek's sister, Laura, had looked like a wolf in death. Maybe eventually he would look like that. And if Allison saw him, she would think he looked beautiful.

And not like the monster he changed into now.

"We should go," he said.

"We haven't looked for Jackson at all," she said, looking guilty. "Let me call Lydia." She pulled her phone out of her pocket. "Uh-oh. My reception is bad here. If my parents call her house, she won't be able to patch me in."

Suddenly he smelled smoke—the tangy odor of wood smoke, forest smoke. It was faint, not the firestorm of his dream. People were allowed to have fires in the preserve. Maybe Jackson had built it for warmth.

He glanced down at the WMP map. He couldn't tell if the fire was near Jackson. Maybe Derek would be able to trace it, but Scott didn't know enough about tracking using his wolf senses, at least while he was in human form.

Little fires can become big ones, he thought, a thrill of panic skittering up his spine as once again he thought about his dream. Flames, all around him. Then the Alpha. And then, in real life, the wolf.

Then his phone rang. It was Stiles.

"Stiles," he said, so Allison would know who it was. "What's up?"

"My new best friend and I are at the hospital," Stiles said, twirling the listening end of a stethoscope in a little circle.

So far he had been unable to hypnotize Derek with it. *Nice werewolf, watch the watch . . .* Maybe you needed a real watch to hypnotize people. Or a real person.

He and Derek were loitering in the stairwell of the cardiac wing of the hospital to get better reception for his call to Scott. "And you'll never guess what. You *can* get past hospital security if you steal a white coat out of the storage room and parade around with it and a clipboard."

Derek grunted. He was the one holding the clipboard, but he had passed on wearing a lab coat.

"Because there isn't any hospital security on this floor," Derek muttered.

"He says hi," Stiles added.

"Who? The . . . *guy?*" Scott asked cryptically on the other end of the line.

"The *other* guy," Stiles replied. "Our friend who is so cheerful." He lowered his voice. "*The* guy was awake. I went in to ask him what kind of Jell-O he wanted for dinner and then I asked him what he saw in the window. And he told me he saw a *monster.* Between screams."

Scott was quiet for a moment. Then he said, "Got any more details?"

"No. He wasn't big on talking. Mostly screaming, and you know that brings the nurses. *Sure*, they say they'll be right there when you call for a bedpan, but if you want them to show, you really need to have a breakdown."

"Stiles," Scott said, sounding a little impatient, the way his father did when he began to ramble.

"Yo," Stiles said contritely. "Sorry."

"So how did practice go?" Scott asked.

Stiles covered the phone. "He can't talk about wolfie matters," he reported to Derek.

"Because he's with *her*," Derek said, looking even more dour than usual. Stiles had never realized there were so many degrees of the brood until Derek Hale had come into their lives.

Stiles was about to speak again when he heard Allison's voice in the background. "Oh, tell Stiles we saw a wolf," she was saying.

"You guys saw a *wolf*?" Stiles repeated carefully, looking over at Derek. Derek did a classic double take. He started to grab for the phone, then stopped himself. Stiles knew it was better for all concerned—okay, for Scott—if no one knew that he and Derek were, like, wolf brothers. If Allison heard Scott yakking on the phone with Derek Hale, that would pretty much put the lie to their not being friends.

"There are no wild wolves in California," Derek muttered.

"There are no wild wolves in California," Stiles repeated. He covered the phone again. "So, are there you-know-whats that look like wolves?" he whispered to Derek. Of course, he and Scott knew the answer to that—a big fat yes—but Derek didn't need to know that when they had dug up his sister's body—okay, the top half of her body—she had been a wolf. Not a semi-wolf, like the werewolf looks they'd seen thus far. A full-on *Call of the Wild* wolf.

Derek didn't answer, only glowered at him. Maybe if he gave Derek a sugar cube—or threw him a piece of raw meat—Derek might cheer up. Stiles would have to try that someday. But today wasn't looking good for that.

Then, whipsaw fast, Derek grabbed the phone out of Stiles's hand. It happened so quickly that it took Stiles a moment to process that he was no longer holding the phone.

"Where are you?" Derek growled in an undervoice.

Stiles strained to hear Scott's answer, but Derek had turned his back. Stiles didn't have superenhanced werewolf hearing. He tried to read Derek's body language, but Derek's shoulders were hunched like always, and his free hand was in the pocket of his jacket, like always, pressing the clipboard against his side as if he might crack it in two. So no help there.

"Then get out of there," Derek said between clenched teeth. *"Now."*

He gave the phone back to Stiles and started to go down the stairs. Aware that he was about to speak to dead air, Stiles followed after Derek.

"Where are we going?" he asked.

"*We* aren't going anywhere," Derek replied.

"Hey, you have to take me with you," Scott's annoying little sidekick insisted as Derek stalked out of the hospital. Derek took a tiny bit of satisfaction in the way the human had to trot along to stay abreast. He was sick to death of taking the weaknesses of humans into account while formulating his plans. He respected power, and few humans had any.

The Argents did.

But what he felt for them was not respect.

He wasn't about to tell Stiles about his dream, or the

real fear he felt when Allison and Scott had told Stiles about their encounter with a wolf. There shouldn't have been a wolf. Things were happening that Derek couldn't explain.

"You have to take me with you because I know how to find Scott in the forest," Stiles said.

"So do I," Derek shot back. "I'll scent him out."

"Well, I have an app for that." Stiles waggled his phone. "On this." Derek ignored him. "Which we should at least use to explain why we're there. What are you going to do, jog up to Scott and Allison and say, 'Oh, hi. I was just on my way to grandmother's house with this basket of goodies and I *smelled* you?'"

Derek kept walking, but he had to admit that the kid had a point. He slid a glance at him. "Show me how to use the app."

Stiles made a point of hugging the phone to his chest. "No way are you taking my phone without me," he said.

"Tell me or I'll rip your throat out," Derek snarled at him. Threats like that had produced perfect results in the past—at Derek's command, Stiles had almost cut off his poisoned arm rather than suffer his wrath. Luckily Scott had arrived with the antidote—a bullet he had stolen from Kate Argent. She had a box of ammo filled with Northern Blue Monkshood— wolfsbane. Derek had used the wolfsbane to cure himself.

Just another reason to hate Kate with all his soul.

"No," Stiles said. "Scott's my best friend, and you're not telling me everything."

I had a nightmare, Derek thought, and huffed to himself. There was no way he was telling Stiles that. Werewolves didn't share information with humans, ever.

Except for him, Derek Hale. He had shared information with a human. He hadn't meant to.

And the results had been disastrous.

"All right," he said. "We'll take your Jeep."

Stiles huffed. "Why can't we ever take your car?"

Jackson was lost.

Sensing imminent danger, he had bolted from Gramm's campfire, and now he didn't know where the hell he was. He tried to get a fix with his phone's GPS, but he wasn't getting a signal. Now he was scrambling over large tree roots and ducking low-lying branches, searching for a path, some partiers, anything. He had no idea why he'd gotten so spooked, and he was trying not to second-guess his decision to leave. Jackson had a gift for reading signals, which was one of the reasons he was so good at lacrosse. Sometimes he just knew which way to run, where the ball would land. It hadn't taken much to notice the difference in Scott McCall's performance, but he seemed to be the only person on the team who had figured out that Scott was on some kind of drug.

Or something.

He pressed his fingertips against the back of his neck, where those nasty scratches were. They were tingling or itching or something—he couldn't quite describe it—and that just added to his sense of urgency. Hell with this. He was getting out of the woods and going to spend the night with Lydia. All he'd have to do was tell her about the note and she would forgive him for blowing her off. Maybe.

If he could find his way out.

The sleepless night at that skanky hotel was taking its toll. Slumping against a tree trunk, he tilted back his head to draw in deep breaths. With all the smoke he smelled, he was amazed he hadn't run into anybody yet. Some kids partying. Up there the stars were shining in constellations and the moon was hanging low, but none of it would help him find his way back to his car. He didn't know anything about celestial navigation or any of that Boy Scout stuff. He knew about lacrosse.

Maybe if I call for help, he thought, but he shook his head. With his luck, some loser from school would hear him whining like a baby. He was resourceful. If he could just get his bearings, he'd be fine.

However . . .

He texted Lydia and hoped it went through. Time to mend some fences, or he'd be spending night number two alone.

CHAPTER SEVEN

Standing beside Allison, Scott smelled smoke. His mind rocketed back to his dream, and his wariness made him edgy. But he tried to remind himself that Beacon Hills Preserve allowed campfires. For all he knew, Jackson had built one to keep warm.

He looked down at his phone. The Where's My Phone app appeared to have failed. The map had disappeared.

"Look," he said, showing it to Allison.

"Mine's gone, too." She frowned.

It was complicated looking for someone he couldn't stand. He knew Allison wasn't all that fond of Jackson, either. She had really stood up to him at the bowling alley when he kept dissing Scott's lack of skills.

Then she'd told me to picture her naked. Like I'm doing right now.

"Let's call Lydia and ask her if she's seeing anything," Allison said.

"We'll have to use my phone," Scott said. He handed his phone to Allison. Their fingers brushed and tingles shot through his body. They'd been kissing for hours but each time he touched her it was like the first time ever.

"Yeah, hi, it's me," she said, nodding at Scott to let him know she'd made the connection.

Scott wandered a bit away to give her privacy, or the semblance of it. In reality, he could hear every word of both sides of the conversation. Lydia couldn't see Jackson on the WMP map anymore, either.

Then Lydia said, "Allison, hold on. He just texted me!"

Allison gestured to Scott. "Jackson's texting her right now."

Scott smiled and nodded. Sometimes you could get a text through even if you couldn't get enough bars for a call.

"I'm going to kill him," Lydia said, her voice a mixture of relief and supreme irritation.

"What did he say?" Allison asked.

" *'I'm ok. I just needed some space. Home soon.'* "

Scott was suspicious. That sounded too nice to be Jackson. At least the Jackson he knew. But sometimes guys acted different with their girlfriends.

"What, Lydia?" Allison said. "I didn't catch all that."

Scott heard static. Either his phone or Lydia's was losing reception. He didn't suppose it really mattered. Jackson was accounted for, if not exactly found.

Allison shrugged. "Lydia said he's in the preserve," she said. "But the call went fuzzy after that. I can try calling her back."

"How's my battery power?" he asked.

"Good question." She looked down at the phone. "Uh-oh. You're at twenty percent."

"No big," he said. "I can always charge it later. If he's going home, I guess we might as well, too." He held his breath waiting for her answer.

Her eyes sparkled as she pretended to ponder his suggestion, tapping her chin with her fingertips.

"Well, we can leave the preserve, but if Lydia's covering for me . . ."

She trailed off, leaving the rest to his imagination. She smiled up at him, and he grinned back, using that imagination to picture her naked some more. They kissed again. But then his conscience got the better of him.

"I'd feel better if we left, with that wolf around," Scott said.

"I think that wolf liked us," Allison countered. "But you're right. We shouldn't push our luck." She dimpled. "I'm going to think of this as one of our special spots."

Wow, Scott thought. *Awesome.*

Then she rose up and kissed him again. She curled her fingers in his hair and he did the same. Her hair was so silky. He didn't want the kiss to ever end, but he ended it first, and took her hand.

He smelled the smoke again, a little stronger, and another little fillip of anxiety tapped at him. Not fear per se, just a reminder to be careful.

They started heading back out of the dense woods in the direction of Allison's car. He held back a branch for her and she ducked beneath it. Moonlight shimmered on her face.

And something changed.

Something in him.

He felt it, almost like the skin on his face was too tight. His nails were pushing against his fingers.

I'm changing, he thought. *No!*

After she passed, he let go of the branch and dropped to one knee, pretending to tie his shoe. In reality, he was examining his nails. Yes, he'd been right. They were growing, the ends savagely pointed. He pressed the pad of his thumb against his canine tooth. It was definitely longer.

No. No, stop, he ordered himself. *This can't be happening.*

He peered up through his lashes at Allison's back. She had just realized he wasn't right behind her and she was going to turn around. He pulled his head down lower, and forced himself to breathe slowly. His heart was pounding. What the hell was he going to do?

"Scott?" Allison said.

"Tying my shoe," he managed to say. He clenched his jaw, feeling the jut of his wolf teeth against his lips. *Get it together.*

"Are you okay?" she asked him.

His sight went red. He kept his gaze downward; in his line of vision, he saw her boots, glowing scarlet, walking toward him. *I didn't kill with the Alpha,* he reminded himself. *Even if I change, I won't hurt her. I swear I won't.*

But if she saw him . . .

"Hey?" she said. Her soft voice was like a clanging bell ringing against his eardrums.

He balled his fists. She was close, so close. Could she see his wolf ears? No. She'd have been screaming by then.

"Scott?" she said, with a bit more concern, and he

watched her start to dip down toward him, bathed in red, so she could look him in the face.

And his nails retracted. He checked his teeth with his tongue. Normal human teeth. He touched his right ear. Fine.

He was no longer seeing everything in red. He rose, hoping to God that his eyes weren't glowing, nearly knocking heads with her. She laughed and brushed his cheek with her lips. He kissed her back, trying to act normal.

Which I'm not, he thought fiercely. *I'm so not normal.*

They laced fingers and walked on. The sun was nearly down. It wasn't a full moon tonight; at least he had that on his side.

"I wondered what happened with the detective," she said. "Poor Lydia. She was so worried about Jackson. He could have at least checked in earlier."

"Yeah." Scott couldn't tell her that he wasn't convinced Jackson was okay. The fact that Jackson had texted Lydia but she hadn't actually heard his voice was still preying on his mind. Besides, he didn't want to suggest that they keep looking for Jackson. All he wanted to do was get her back to her car and keep her safe.

From the wild wolf, and the darkness, and himself.

I shouldn't have texted Lydia that I'm okay, Jackson thought, catching his breath, *because I'm not.*

Sure, he'd left Gramm standing in the shadows. He had

just turned and split without saying a word, because Jackson Whittemore didn't explain himself to anyone. Well, except to Lydia, to keep her happy. It was *so* much easier to deal with Lydia when she was happy. Plus . . . benefits.

But now he was lost.

And things still felt wrong.

He'd thought maybe the detective (if he really was a detective) had brought someone along and he was so mad at himself for taking such a huge risk. It was just . . . the picture of that guy looked so much like him. And not Photoshopped, unless the detective had bothered to make it look like an old picture.

That's not so hard, Jackson thought. *Any dork in Graphic Design 1A can do it.*

He took the picture out of his pocket and aimed his flashlight at it. His eyes, his jawline. Was it his real dad?

Biological father, he corrected himself, but something deep down still said "real."

His parents had made him see a therapist a couple of times during the summer before ninth grade. He had been spending every waking hour at lacrosse practice, and had just gotten back from a private camp, in fact, when one evening, just out of the blue, they informed him that the next day he was going to see Dr. Taggert.

"Just for a checkup," his dad had said. And his mom had smiled her tight little smile that meant things were not totally okay with her, and given Jackson a reassuring nod. Like he was some kind of moron who wouldn't notice that they were trying to pass off this "checkup" as something normal.

He spent the entire night tossing and turning, wondering if he had said or done something that had thrown down a red flag. He went back over every single moment he could remember at camp. He'd hung with a tight bunch of guys he'd known from other camps, and yeah, okay, there were a couple of boys who tried to mix it up with him and he'd set them straight. But that was normal stuff, guy stuff. Guys who played lacrosse were tough—they had to be. Lacrosse was a very aggressive sport. Some people didn't know that, and sometimes, watching their first lacrosse practice, they got freaked out.

It had to be something like that.

But he didn't say anything about going to see the therapist because part of him didn't want to hear that they were somehow disappointed in him. He wondered about it all night—he wouldn't say that he *worried*; it was just on his mind—and he was feeling draggy when his mom drove him to the office.

They went into together, everyone sitting in big comfy chairs. There was a wall of framed college degrees and a mountain landscape like you'd see in a hotel room. Jackson's mom kept saying over and over that everything was fine; they just wanted to make sure that Jackson was ready for high school. It felt like the two adults were speaking in some kind of code that Jackson didn't know. And that they knew he didn't know it, and were talking right in front of him *about* him and weren't telling him.

That was the first visit. It turned out they had to go again, so Jackson could talk to Dr. Taggert alone. At first Jackson thought that was a dirty trick, but then he wondered if he'd said or done something wrong during the session with his mom present that had triggered the request for a private chat. It pissed him off because the appointment was scheduled during a scrimmage he and his best friend, Danny, had set up.

His mom drove him again but this time she stayed in the waiting room, head bowed over her e-reader. Dr. Taggert just chitchatted with him forever, about his hobbies, his interests, his life, which made him even more freaked out, and then the dude started talking about being adopted.

He told Jackson that different adopted kids felt differently about being adopted. For some, it was a heart-wrenching loss, a wound that never healed. For others, it was no big deal. They were philosophical about it and just moved on with their lives.

Jackson figured that philosophical was the way to go. Only wimps sat around and cried about their lot in life.

Others kicked ass on the field.

"So how do you feel about being adopted, Jackson?" Dr. Taggert had asked him.

"I've got nothing," Jackson had replied. "I don't think about it."

Dr. Taggert unwrapped a peppermint and popped it into his mouth. He had an amazing amount of candy in his office. Not an apple or a banana in sight.

"Everybody thinks about it at least a little bit. How about you, Jackson? What are you thinking right now?"

Jackson had looked blankly at Dr. Taggert, then glanced at his wall of diplomas.

I'm thinking that I'm not telling some guy who went to a

bunch of state schools anything, Jackson had silently replied. Even though it completely weirded him out that his parents had decided to send him to a psychologist, he was insulted that they'd gone so low rent. That was not the Whittemore way. It was the best for the best.

"I'm fine. I'm good," Jackson had said aloud.

"That's really great," Dr. Taggert had replied. "That's great to hear, Jackson. Because . . . sometimes little questions or small concerns that we have about issues in our lives can start to grow. Like weeds. They can manifest in different ways, affecting our grades, athletic performance . . ." He'd looked at Jackson. "You're on your way to high school, and we want to start out on a level playing field, yes?"

And in that moment, Jackson realized the reason he was there. His parents wanted to make sure he did well in high school. "Excellence" was the Whittemore family motto, and this was their insurance policy to keep things excellent. What, hadn't he been performing at capacity? Was there something he'd messed up on? He tried to think through everything he'd done in the last year. Middle school was history, and he'd gotten straight A's. Captained his youth division summer lacrosse team, hung out, read *To Kill a Mockingbird* for freshman English, stuff like that.

He felt a tightening in his stomach, the same way he felt when someone scored a point off him. Or he missed some really obvious answers on a test.

He was here because his parents didn't want him to screw up. Which meant that they thought he *might* screw up. He stared at Dr. Taggert's big glass bowl of peppermints like it was a crystal ball and he could see his future. There was no way he was going to screw up *anything*. He had everything under total control.

He grabbed a peppermint to have something to do. Fill the silence. But he didn't unwrap it. He just held it in his palm.

"Jackson?" Dr. Taggert had queried. "Is there something you'd like to say?"

Why don't my parents just set three hundred dollars on fire and be done with it? Jackson had thought. *If that's what this is about, it's a total waste.*

"It's all good," he'd told the shrink.

But now, in the woods, he was turned around. The marks on the back of his neck were bugging him and he put his hand over them as he stopped and looked up at the treetops. Who could tell one tree from another?

Where the hell am I? he thought. He looked down at his superexpensive smartphone and swore at it. All that money and he still had crappy reception. They really needed to get more cell towers in Beacon Hills. Maybe his text hadn't gone through. If she'd texted back, he hadn't gotten it.

Maybe she's punishing me for not showing last night, he thought. It wasn't as if it was their first night alone in his house or anything. His parents traveled a lot. And *she* had done the same thing more than once—found something to pout about and stayed home. It wasn't as if they had to seize the moment on those few and far occasions when there were moments to be had. They had lots of moments. Great ones, if he did say so himself.

And I could be home right now having another one, if I hadn't fallen for this total scam.

Still, the guy in the picture looked like they could be related. Maybe like father and son.

Maybe Gramm had had something to sell. Maybe Jackson's alarm bells had gone off because there was some predator in the forest. Where there was one mountain lion, there could be two.

Or something else altogether.

"Hey?" Jackson called. "Gramm?"

He ran his flashlight over the trees as he waited for an answer. He didn't know how far he'd run. It felt as if he'd been going in a circle.

The beam of his light landed on something poking out of a tree trunk. It looked too straight to be a branch.

He walked up and squinted at it. Long, straight, wood. It was an arrow. Curious, he tried to pull it out. By the looks of the wood around the hole it had made, it was fresh.

Is someone doing archery around here? he wondered. Then a feeling of icy dread squeezed his heart. *Are they shooting at me?*

He heard a funny little screech, like something that should be scary, only wasn't because it was too soft and high pitched. It was definitely an animal, and it sounded like it was on the ground.

Giving the arrow another anxious glance, he ran his flashlight beam over the ground. There was still a little daylight out, but the trees grew so closely together that they blocked out the setting sun. He kept thinking about Gramm, wondering if he'd made a mistake to walk away.

Yeah, right. First he makes me spend the night in a trashy motel and then he meets me in the middle of a forest. If he's really got something for me, he knows how to find me. And I'm setting the terms of when and where we meet.

Gramm had caught Jackson in a weak moment. He hadn't thought about being adopted in, like, forever. Until Scott McCall started showing some skills on the field and Jackson got to wondering about his own physicality. Did he run as fast as he did because of his father? Was there anything he should know about himself, like did people in his family have trick ankles, or—

This is a bunch of crap, he thought. Things like that would *never* have occurred to him, except that his parents took him to see that fraud, Dr. Taggert, back when he was younger and more impressionable.

He heard the screech again and looked back down at the ground. Bushes ahead and to the right shifted and jittered, and Jackson slowly crept up on them. The screech sounded again.

"It's just some stupid animal," he said aloud, but when he reached the bushes, he cautiously pushed them this way and that, inspecting them.

Two black eyes peered up at him. Startled, he jumped back slightly, then crept back toward it to have another look. It was a baby bird, a hawk, by its look. It gazed directly up at him and screeched again.

Jackson studied it. Maybe it had hurt itself and couldn't

fly away. Or it had fallen out of its nest and was too young to fly. Had the mama bird abandoned it?

Then it opened its wings as far as it could, hemmed in as it was by the bushes. Jackson reached in and broke off some of the branches on the right. The bird made a terrible racket and fluttered its wings.

"Hold on. I'm helping you," he said.

Maybe he should leave it. Maybe this way nature's way. If there was something wrong with it, somebody higher on the food chain should have a crack at it, right?

Pursing his lips, he broke off some branches on the left side of the bird. The bird tried to peck him and he chuckled at its ferocity.

"You want me just to leave you?" he asked it.

"Hey," said a voice behind him. Jackson turned.

CHAPTER EIGHT

Standing behind Jackson was a striking girl with blond hair about his age, wearing a lot of kohl around her golden brown eyes. She wore a silver jacket with a fuzzy hood and a pair of jeans. He didn't recognize her, which meant that if she went to his school, she was beneath his notice.

"Hey," he replied. He gestured with his head toward the tree. "Is that your arrow?"

She jerked, probably looking as startled as he had when he'd seen it. She moved away from the tree, toward him.

"No. Is someone doing archery?" She swiveled around. "Are we going to get, like, shot?"

"I don't know. Hey, do you know how to get out of here?" he asked. "I'm in the parking lot."

"Yeah, sure," she said. "What are you doing?"

"Come look," he invited.

She minced toward him. He caught himself touching the wounds on the back of his neck with his right hand as he held back the branches with his left. The bird started going completely psycho. "I think it's trapped."

She was wearing the same Vera Wang perfume Lydia wore. Pricey. "Oh, it's a hawk," she said. "A predator."

It sounded like a strange thing to say. She took a couple of steps back, and the bird seemed to calm down the merest little bit. Jackson was about to leave it so he could get back to the parking lot and find Lydia, when the bird screeched again and he looked down at it.

"It thinks you're its daddy," she said, grinning at him.

"Well, I'm not." He watched the bird bobbing its head up and down, up and down, like some kind of cartoon. Squatting down, he broke away more branches, half expecting it to take off. It kept bobbing and screeching, and the girl looked upward.

"Mama's not coming," she said. "It's probably hungry."

"Do you go to Beacon Hills?" Jackson asked her.

Her lips curved upward in a little grin. She shook her head. "But I'm here with some people. I can take you to the lot and then I should get back. I'll be missed."

Jackson looked down at the hawk. Stupidly, he was concerned about it.

"You said it might be hungry," he ventured. "These things eat meat, right?"

"Yes, so unless you have a dead mouse on you, there's not much you can do for it." She shifted her weight. "I kind of have to make this quick."

"What's your name?" he asked her.

"Cassie. You?"

"Jackson." He realized he was waiting to see if she recognized his name. But she'd already said she didn't go to Beacon Hills.

"Hold on a sec," he said.

Jackson yanked out more of the undergrowth on either side of the excited bird, really going for it. The bird flapped its wings and took off, aiming straight for Jackson's head. Jackson cried out and flopped onto his back, and the bird curved upward, soaring into the trees. Cassie burst out laughing and Jackson did, too. It was just so crazy after a horrible, crazy twenty-four hours.

"Here, let me help you up," she said, reaching out a hand. He took it. Her grip was amazingly strong. He pushed himself to his feet and suddenly he was standing facing her. She was tall, but not as tall as he was.

She had a funny look on her face, like she was about to say something but wasn't sure if she should. He couldn't read it and he surreptitiously checked his nose for souvenirs by pretending to cough and ran his tongue along his teeth. Everything was fine. But he didn't need to be so careful. She hadn't even noticed. She was looking at the ground, and Jackson looked down, too, half expecting to find another baby bird or something at her feet. But there was nothing.

"I don't want to keep you," he said, hinting. She was pretty, but he had a life to get back to.

She went very still, almost not moving. Something was up with her, but he didn't know what it was. And he didn't have time to find out. He'd already done his good deed for the day.

"You said you were in a hurry," he reminded her.

She inhaled a deep breath and held it. Then she let it out slowly. "Yeah. Come on."

"Oh. Do you have a phone?" he asked. "Mine isn't

working. Which is ironic, because it's a very expensive phone."

"I'm sure it is," she replied. That confused him. He had no idea what she meant by that, so he just waited for her answer. "I don't have a phone, actually," she said. But her face went red, and he knew she was lying. Maybe it was a cheap one, and she was embarrassed to let him use it.

In a few minutes it wouldn't matter. He'd be back in his car and on his way to extreme makeup passion with Lydia. The sooner he was out of here the better. And he was *never* coming back here *or* getting scammed by some two-bit guy who thought he'd siphon off some of that great Whittemore money. He'd watch *The Notebook* with Lydia for twenty-four hours straight before he did anything this insane again.

"Thanks for doing this," he said to her. "I appreciate it."

She went silent again. Then she turned her back and said, "No problem."

They began to walk, she in front of him, and he behind. He smelled her perfume . . . and smoke. He jerked, anxious that they might run into Gramm again.

"We're not heading in the direction of any campfires, are we?" He tried to sound casual.

"No," she said. "Parking lot." She looked over her shoulder at him. "What kind of car do you drive?"

"A Porsche," he said proudly.

"Figures," she murmured. They walked on, she in front. Jackson pulled out his phone to check his reception. Still no service. *Damn.*

Cassie kept leading the way, moving aside branches that she held for him. He grinned to himself, comparing how Lydia would never have done such a thing, but he was also beginning to wonder how long the hike back was going to take. He must have gotten himself turned way around.

"We're going the right way, right?" he said to her back.

"Uh-huh," she replied. "Trust me."

At the Argents' house, all the new weapons were put away in the garage. All that beautiful ammo. Those lovely guns. Kate still hadn't figured out if they had anything new in their arsenal, and Chris wasn't saying. He was finishing checking a box of crossbow bolts. *Crossbow bolts*, for heaven's sake. Why bother with Robin Hood when there were rocket launchers to be had?

Kate liked to think that they were ready for anything, but she knew all too well that where werewolves were involved, you couldn't get too cocky. Take their present situation. When she'd come back to Beacon Hills, she'd figured she'd pop into town, kill whatever was slinking around, put some more notches in her belt, and that would be that.

Then things got complicated, and she was more than willing to blame Derek Hale for all of it. Some werewolf *he* was—couldn't even figure out the identity of the new Alpha. And as long as Derek was alive, he could get her in major trouble, by implicating her in the fire. Sad to say, she was surrounded by people who still lived by that outdated code. In her opinion, the only good werewolf was a dead werewolf. And as for those so-called normal Hales who had died in the unfortunate electrical fire in their house?

Better safe than sorry.

"So when is Allison coming home tonight?" she asked Chris as he set the alarm code in the entryway to the garage. She watched over his shoulder to see if he was changing the password. Yes. To "SILVER." Not too original, but her brother had colored inside the lines for so long she would have expected nothing more from him.

"She's spending the night at her friend's," Chris told her. "They're working on an English project."

She snorted. "Chris, really? This *is* the same Allison who cut school and stole a condom out of my bag, right? I mean, I love my niece, but what's the saying about giving someone enough rope? They hang themselves?"

To her surprise, he didn't take the bait and start arguing with her. He just gave her one of those enigmatic smiles that used to drive her crazy while they were growing up and walked into the kitchen, where Victoria, his wife, was putting the finishing touches on dinner.

Kate snitched a cherry tomato out of the salad and popped it into her mouth. "How about you, Vicky?" she asked her sister-in-law. "Do you think Allison's studying with a friend?"

Victoria Argent smiled coldly back at her and checked the oven. The aroma of baked chicken tantalized Kate's senses.

"Allison has made some poor choices lately," Victoria conceded, "but we didn't want her home for the weapons delivery."

"So, you can tell her to come home now," Kate said. "Everything's stashed." She pulled out her cell phone. "Should I call Allison and see how her study date is going?"

Scott kept monitoring himself on the walk to Allison's car. The hike back to it seemed longer than their original trek, and he began to wonder if they had gone the wrong way. But mingled with his anxiety was real wonder at the beauty of the woods in the setting sun. All his senses were in play; he could smell mushrooms and damp earth, and Allison's shampoo and perfume. The smell of the smoke was fainter now, and he scented rain in the clouds. He could smell the weather. How cool was that?

He saw the blue glow of the stars, and a milky ring around the moon appeared in the sky. What was it about the full moon that made him change? Was all this magic? Did he actually believe in magic?

When he looked at Allison, the answer was yes.

There was her car, parked exactly where they had left it. He heaved a sigh of relief, chased by a little thrill as she looked over her shoulder at him. In the world of high school, cars were like portable bedrooms. Except he didn't want their first time to be in a car.

Or maybe I'm being too picky, he thought, as, still gazing invitingly at him, she reached into her purse. To get the keys, he assumed.

"Huh," she said, and dug around some more. Then she held her purse open and peered inside. "I don't see my keys."

He woke his phone up and shined its illuminated display window into her purse, making a silent inventory of the contents—lip gloss, pens, her phone, a leather wallet, a tiny notebook, what looked like more makeup.

But no keys.

Her forehead furrowed, she looked up at him, then dug around some more. He rewound the night in his head, trying to remember where he'd last seen her keys.

"I took them, right?" she murmured. Then she put her hand around the driver's door handle and opened it. She smiled hopefully. "Maybe I left them in the ignition." She sat down in her seat and reached forward. Felt around.

"They're not there, Scott," she said nervously.

"Maybe you dropped them on the ground when you got out." He started scanning the area around the door, figuring he was too close to her—making it too risky—to use his enhanced vision. Aside from chancing discovery of his weirdly glowing eyes, he didn't want to initiate a shift he couldn't pull himself back from.

No keys.

Increasing the search area, he moved back a couple of feet and squatted down, pushing away ferns and underbrush, anticipating a metallic glint. Behind him, Allison was examining the floor of the car and feeling between the seats. He could hear her muttering under her breath, walking herself through her actions. Everything was kind of a blur for him—he'd been so distracted just being alone with her—so maybe it was like that for her, too.

"They're not here," she said. "Oh, God, Scott. What did I do with them?"

A breeze blew her hair as she climbed back out of the car and faced him. And the wind brought the stronger odor of smoke with it. As if the fire had grown . . . or there was a second fire.

His heartbeat picked up.

Don't wolf, he ordered himself.

"Let's backtrack," she said. "I must have dropped them when we first started out. I had my phone out." She started walking back the way they had just come. "I looked for my gloves." She stopped and opened her purse. "No. I didn't have them in my purse. They were in my jacket pocket." She brightened and put her hand into her pocket. "They're probably . . . not there." Her face fell. "Scott . . ."

"I'll call Stiles," he said. "He can come get us."

"That's not the problem," she said. "Well, not the immediate problem. I can't leave my car here."

Scott realized they were focused on two different issues. She wanted to find her keys, and he wanted to get her out of the preserve. He opened his mouth to explain, but he reminded himself that he was dealing with Allison Argent. She would probably laugh at him if he told her he was feeling protective.

He couldn't let that matter.

"Stiles can get you and take you to Lydia's," he repeated, "and I'll stay here and look for your keys. When I find them, I'll drive your car to Lydia's." He looked down at his phone. The charge had gone down to 15 percent. He reminded himself that once he had found the keys, he could charge his phone in her car.

Aware that she hadn't responded, he gazed up expectantly at her. She shook her head and gave him a mock-stern look. "I'm not leaving you out here while I'm all cozy." She made a face. "And while I'm not with you."

Scott wanted to pinch himself. She really did like him.

"Then you wait in the car," he said.

"No. Two sets of eyes are definitely better than one." She cocked her head and raised a brow. "It's the wolf, isn't it?"

"What?" he asked, his voice rising shrilly. He cleared his throat. "What?" he said in a lower, more manly register.

"You're afraid that the wolf will attack us." She broke eye contact as she studied the ground, circling the car. "I don't know a whole lot about wolves, but I do remember something I saw on a show somewhere. They're very shy. They don't attack unless provoked."

He lowered his head and let his wolf vision take over so they could find the keys more quickly and leave. If he worked hard at keeping his head turned away, she wouldn't be able to see his eyes.

"So how do you explain the fact that that wolf just walked right up to us? That was definitely not shy," he argued.

"Maybe it's not a wolf. Maybe it was something else," she said, and he jerked, startled.

"Like what?"

She thought a moment. "Well, I think there are dogs that look very wolflike. Have you ever seen anything like that at the vet clinic?"

"Nothing like what we saw," he insisted. "I swear that was a wolf."

"Well, maybe it was just passing through. I'll bet we could have petted it if we'd wanted to. Not that I would have," she said. "I'm not stupid."

"I know," he said. He didn't want her to think he was insulting her intelligence. It was so hard to carry such a deep secret. *Why* did her father have to be a hunter? Why did there have to be hunters at all?

"Any luck?" he asked, trying to change the subject, but it was a lame attempt. If she'd found her keys, she would have said something.

"They're definitely not here." She raised her head. "Scott, I *can't* leave here without my keys."

"I'll call Stiles and ask him to come help us," he said.

"I was hoping to have some time alone," she murmured. "But, well, I *do* need my keys." She sniffed the air. "There's more smoke. Someone must be having a bonfire."

"Yeah, maybe."

"Well, that means there are other people nearby. So the animals will keep away. The *wolf*," she added, in case he didn't catch her drift. "And maybe we can get some other people to help."

But then he had a thought. "Allison," he said carefully, "maybe someone took the keys."

She laughed and shook her head. "Who would do that?"

"But what if someone did?" he asked. "Maybe just for a prank, or something?"

"That would be . . . really mean," she said hotly. "I don't know anyone who would do that."

You're new here, he thought.

He tried to sniff the air without her noticing, to see if he could tell if anyone had been near her car. Then her phone rang, and as she pulled it out of her purse, he inhaled more deeply. He wasn't spectacular at picking out scents— although he had smelled the blood on Laura Hale's dead body, both in the morgue and in her grave—and he wasn't having any luck now with trying to smell humans who might have opened the car while they'd been out of sight.

CHAPTER NINE

Hello?" Allison said into the phone.

"Oh, good, you're out of the bathroom," Lydia replied in a falsely bright voice. Allison hadn't put the call on speaker, but Scott could hear her perfectly. "Your aunt's on the line. I told her I'd have you pick up on the extension."

Allison's eyes grew huge. Scott heard her heart stutter a couple of beats as she licked her lips and put a smile on her face. "Hey, Aunt Kate. Hi. Yeah, everything's great."

Without revealing that he was doing it, Scott listened in. Why was her aunt checking up on Allison? He'd had a close call with Kate Argent the night he'd stayed for dinner and stolen that bullet. His mind rewound through the entire horrible evening, from her dad needling him about drinking and smoking pot to Stiles's texts that Derek was dying. Scott had gone into the guest room "to use the bathroom" when in reality he'd been searching for the ammunition she'd used to give Derek a lethal dose of wolfsbane poisoning. He'd found it, and taken one to give to Derek, who had used it for his cure.

But Kate had noticed that the bag had been tampered with and accused him of stealing something from her—what, she hadn't been exactly sure—and she had ordered him to prove his innocence by taking everything out of his pockets. But just in the nick of time, Allison had confessed that she'd gone into Kate's bag to get a condom.

For me. To be with me. To have sex.

With me.

Despite his jitters, couldn't hide his delighted, goofy smile. What would have happened if Allison hadn't taken it? What if he'd had to empty his pockets, and Kate had seen the bullet? Was it possible to be completely freaked out and happy at the exact same time?

Yes. And he was living proof of that.

"I just wanted to make sure everything's going okay," her aunt was saying on the phone.

"Things are fine," Allison replied, staring at Scott. He could hear her heartbeat. It was in overdrive. She put her finger to her lips, begging him to be silent, and he was a little bit insulted. Obviously he understood that Aunt Kate should not know she was with him. Then he reminded himself that Allison was nervous, and he gave her an encouraging smile.

Oh, yeah, things are great, Scott thought. *We're stuck in the preserve without Allison's car keys.*

"You don't need anything from the house? Don't need me to swing by?" Kate pressed.

Allison looked as if she was going to faint. "Nope," she said. "I'm all set."

"Hey, Allison," Lydia said on the other line. "My mom wants our help setting the table. If you don't mind."

"No problem. Be right there," Allison said.

"I don't think I've had the pleasure of speaking to your mother," Kate said. "Hey, what—"

"Allison," said another voice. Scott freaked. Oh, God, it was Allison's father. Involuntarily, he shrank back into the shadows, as if her father could see right through the phone. Allison was wigging out, too. Scott could hear her heart thundering.

"Have a nice time with your friend, honey," Mr. Argent said.

"Thank you, Dad," Allison replied.

There was a click as the call was disconnected. Then Lydia called back.

"Is she for real?" she cried. "What is *up* with your aunt?"

"I'm sorry," Allison murmured. She was speaking to Lydia, but looking straight at Scott. Why was she apologizing? It was his fault that she'd been grounded. He'd talked her into skipping school.

"She's . . . overprotective. She hasn't seen me in a year and I think she still pictures me as a little girl, you know?"

Because last year you were only sixteen instead of seventeen, Scott thought. *Hardly a little girl.*

"I could see your father acting that way," Lydia replied. "Well, anyway, I think we can rest a little easier. Your family has checked up on you, and your dad obviously trusts you, so it's all good."

"Yeah," Allison said, and it was obvious to Scott that not

being honest with her father bothered her. Scott still didn't know if Allison was aware of the world of werewolves and hunters. It hadn't exactly come up in conversation.

Then Scott had a thought, not his favorite, and he couldn't share it. But if Jackson was on his way out of the preserve, maybe he, Scott, could track him and ask him for help. To look for the keys, to take Allison home, something.

The idea of asking Jackson for a favor made him wince. Jackson would make sure he got payback, and if he knew that Allison and Scott had both snuck out to be together, he'd be able to get them in trouble if he felt like it.

But then he'd get in trouble, too. At least we didn't go to that cheap motel.

Or, wait. We did.

Everything was getting too complicated.

He realized Allison was still on the phone with Lydia, and resumed his eavesdropping.

"I have a sort of a problem," Allison said to Lydia. "I can't find my car keys."

After a beat, Lydia said, "You're kidding, right?"

"I think I dropped them . . . someplace," Allison confessed. She brightened. "What about a locksmith?"

"They'll have to check with the person the car is registered to," Lydia said. "I know this from personal experience. Not that I've ever lost my keys, but I have a friend who did."

Allison sagged and bit her lower lip as she looked at Scott. "Then we have to find them."

Back to square one. Scott tried to smile reassuringly as Allison disconnected. Then she slid her arms around him. She leaned her head against his chest and gazed up at him.

"This isn't the most romantic Friday night." She wrinkled her nose.

"I'm having a great time," he said, kissing her.

Where the hell are we? Jackson thought. They had been trekking through the preserve like two people on a frickin' safari or something. Jackson could smell smoke so strong he kept expecting to run into Gramm's campfire again. Then he realized it was Friday night and people were partying. This wasn't his kind of deal. He was damn lucky there was no lacrosse game tonight, or he would be in serious trouble with Coach. Now that his "adventure" was almost over, he couldn't believe that he'd blown off Lydia like this. He was just totally overcranked lately.

"I don't mean to, um, doubt you," Jackson said to Cassie, "but this is taking awhile, and I need to get home."

She turned around, facing him, and stretched her arms out to the sides. She moved her head from side to side, stretching her neck muscles, and said, "I'll bet you sleep in a nice, big bed."

He smiled. He was flattered, even though he was used to girls coming onto him. He drove a Porsche, wore Hugo Boss. He worked out, and he wasn't bad looking.

"Yeah," he said. "I do."

"We move around a lot," she said. "Sometimes I even sleep in our car. Hopefully soon I can . . . fly away." She mimicked the baby bird. "Wasn't that too funny, how that thing came right at you?"

He chuckled. "If you ever tell anyone I freaked out over a bird . . ." Then he remembered that she wasn't from here, and didn't know anyone he knew. It was fortunate that she knew her way around the preserve.

"Make you a deal," she said. "I don't tell anyone about that, and you don't tell anyone about . . . me."

He frowned, puzzled. "I don't know anything about you."

"No, I mean, don't tell anyone that you saw me. Because . . . I could get in trouble."

"Trouble?" He blinked. "Just for talking to a guy?"

She walked up to him. He could smell her perfume. They were almost the same height. She gazed in his eyes hard, as if she were trying to tell him something. And then she kissed him.

Her lips were soft, and it was an okay kiss, but there was Lydia, and getting out of there. So he didn't diss her by pulling back, but he didn't go for it, either. He knew how to end a kiss without making it seem like he was ending it, and that was what he did.

"That was so nice," she murmured with a blushy little smile. "I haven't ever had a boyfriend. We're always on the ru—go."

She'd been about to say something else. He didn't know what, but he wasn't going to ask. Flirting was nice and all . . . in the right time and place.

Then she started to kiss him again, and he put a hand on her shoulder to stop her. Her face fell, and he wanted to shake her. It was beginning to dawn on him that she might not know the way to the parking lot after all. That she might be messing with him.

"Okay, okay," she said tiredly. She gestured for him to follow her. She pointed. "There's the Porsche," she said. "Sweet ride."

And there about twenty yards below the little hill they stood on was the small parking lot, with his freshly detailed Porsche parked across two spaces, so that no one could ding it.

Finally, he thought, as he pulled out his keys with a sigh of relief. He turned to thank her.

But she wasn't there.

"Hey," he said. "Cassie?"

There was no answer. He looked around, peering into the trees and the shadows surrounding him. It was as if she'd never been beside him. As if she were a ghost.

"Thank you," he called, shaking his head. She was just the most recent in a long list of very weird things that had happened since yesterday morning.

He was halfway to the Porsche when someone stepped from a row of bushes bordering the lot, so that he was between Jackson and his car. The figure was cloaked in darkness, but Jackson made out the silhouette of Hunter Gramm. Jackson faltered when he saw him, but ignored him and headed for the left, to avoid him. Warily, he slid his glance toward the guy, who was watching him.

"Jackson," Gramm said, walking toward him. Jackson still couldn't make out his features. "Hold on. I'm sorry you got spooked. I really do have information for you."

"We're done," Jackson said, without stopping. "You don't know anything about me or my birth family. You're just some scam artist."

He pulled his phone out of his pocket. Reception. Thank God.

"Is that your phone?" Hunter Gramm said.

Jackson jutted out his chin. "Yeah, why?"

Then at last Gramm stepped from the shadows beneath the parking lot light, and Jackson saw that he was wearing a black ski mask.

"Toss it over there," he said. *"Now."*

And that he was holding a gun.

"What's that smoke?" Derek asked as he peered through the windshield of Stiles's Jeep. In the distance, two black plumes rose into the dark sky. He leaned his head out of the window and inhaled the smell. Timber wood.

"I *told* you not to do that," Stiles grumped. Then he said, "Oh. No tongue lolling, sorry. It's just smoke. You can build fires in the preserve." He made a face. "You're not big on smoke. I get that."

"You don't know anything about me, so shut up," Derek said.

"Kinda do," Stiles replied. "Wish I didn't," he said under his breath.

"Just drive," Derek said.

Stiles fell silent and did as Derek said. As they neared the preserve, Stiles looked queasily at Derek and said, "Don't bite me if I tell you bad news." Derek looked over at him, waiting for him to go on. "I've lost Scott's signal."

Derek growled. Stiles held the phone out to him. "We could try yours. Download the app and—"

"I don't have a cell phone," Derek informed him. He hadn't imagined needing one. The reception at his house was practically nil, and he could pretty easily find Scott when he needed him. And aside from the Alpha, Scott McCall was the only person in Beacon Hills he needed to communicate with.

Actually, I don't need to communicate with the Alpha. I just need to kill him.

And he sure as hell didn't want anyone tracking him with a cell phone.

Stiles muttered to himself. Derek kept his eye on the twin plumes of smoke.

Which were quickly joined by a third.

"Is that normal?" Derek asked Stiles. "So many fires?"

"I don't know, but I'm guessing yes," Stiles said. "I'm not usually in a group that does stuff like that on Friday nights. Before Scott had a girlfriend, we did, like, multiplayer games, hung out, watched movies."

Derek snorted.

"Yeah, well, Mr. Werewolf guy, I don't exactly picture you attending homecoming, either."

I almost did, Derek thought as he clenched his jaw and glared at Stiles. "Drive faster."

Bad vibes were running through Derek as thoroughly as the volts from Kate's cattle prod. If someone had asked him to explain what was bothering him, he wouldn't have been able to explain his reasons point by point. But he was

a werewolf, and he had animal instincts, and his gut was telling him that there was something wrong.

Stiles was taking the curves on squealing tires. Still, if
Derek shifted, he could run faster. As he was considering it,
Stiles made a sharp turn and barreled onto a narrow road.
Derek realized with a start that it was the back road to his
house—a private road. But it had somehow been mapped
and put into data banks. That made him feel violated. The
world was shrinking. When the code had been created,
hunters had ridden horses and used crossbows. Now they
drove around in Hummers and used submachine guns. And
broke the code without blinking twice.

But they will pay for that.

Stiles drove on the Hale road for a while, then pulled
over. He looked at Derek, then punched a number on his
phone. He nodded.

"I've got the signal back. Scott's ringing," he said.
"And . . . ringing." He moved his head left, right. Trying
to get good reception, Derek understood. He wanted to
grab the phone and talk to Scott himself, but he let the
idiot do it.

"Maybe his phone's dead," Stiles said.

"Then I'll scent him out. My nose doesn't die," Derek
grumbled.

"What if you have a cold?" Stiles asked him, and Derek
realized he wasn't trying to be sarcastic. He was genuinely
curious. Derek didn't care. Stiles could stay curious.

Derek got out of the Jeep; then he raised his head and
inhaled. So much smoke. He hated the smell. Clenching his

fists inside the pockets of his black leather jacket, he started to walk. Behind him, Stiles clambered out and caught up with him.

"Why are you so worried about Scott?" Stiles demanded as he put on a hoodie. "Oh, I know, the Alpha and all, but—"

Derek had had it. He grabbed Stiles by the front of his sweatshirt and slammed him against a tree trunk. Stiles grunted hard, and Derek got into his face.

"Yes, 'the Alpha *and all*,'" he said through clenched teeth. "Are you really this stupid? You've seen what the Alpha is capable of. You *know* that mountain lion had nothing to do with what's going on."

"Yeah, yeah, I do," Stiles said. His face was ashen. He held up his hands. "Don't take this the wrong way, but, well, it's like you're PMSing, dude. I mean, you're even crankier than usual. Which, even you have to admit, is off the charts on a good day."

"I don't know why I don't just kill you," Derek said, letting his enhanced vision take over, so that Stiles would see his eyes.

"And I sincerely hope you'll keep asking yourself the big questions," Stiles said. "Seriously, man, I'm not the enemy, okay?"

You're too weak to be my enemy, Derek thought. But Stiles could easily become an enemy. One word spoken to the wrong person, and the sheriff's son could destroy him. Derek knew exactly how that could go down.

Derek let go of him and kept walking. The smoke was

blanketing the other forest smells, and he couldn't help but feel that it was deliberate. Then the moonlight shone down on a car, and his heart nearly stopped. He recognized that car. It belonged to Allison Argent.

But the scent that was covering it belonged to the Alpha.

CHAPTER TEN

O nce the sun had gone down, the temperature had plummeted, too. Allison had retrieved a heavier jacket from her car. But she was still shivering as the two of them retraced their steps through the forest. Their breaths were like huge ghosts floating around them. Scott hoped they would run into one of the campfires so she could warm up. Or they could just make their own, if it looked as if they were going to be stuck looking for a while.

He walked in front of her, alert, cautious. Even though she was working hard to keep up, he could tell she was getting tired. He didn't know what to do.

"Scott." She tugged on his wrist, and he turned quickly. She waggled his hand and caught her lower lip between her teeth. "I need to take a break," she said. "I'm so cold."

He put his arms around her and molded her against his chest. Shutting his eyes against the tide of pleasure that washed over him, he nestled her head beneath his chin. Her knitted cap was scratchy as she settled trustingly against him, and he ran his fingers through the strands of her hair. What was the worst that could happen if they just gave up? Maybe Lydia would lie for them, say that she and Allison had driven to the preserve to study, or pick up Jackson, or something. Sure, the Argents would be angry with her, but not half as angry if they knew that she'd lied to them so she could be with Scott.

Sighing, he was about to broach the subject when she leaned her head back and kissed his jawline. She cupped her hand around the side of his face, bringing his mouth toward hers. She kissed him long and slow, and he had the presence of mind to check his fingernails. So far.

So very, very good.

Stiles was gasping for breath by the time Derek finally stopped charging through the underbrush. He remembered when Scott had suffered from his terrible asthma attacks—that was all gone now, thanks to the Bite—and his own hideous panic attacks when his mom had died. Not being able to catch your breath really sucked.

But at least he could pant to death in the presence of warmth. Derek had halted at the base of a banked campfire. There was no fire, but the embers were still glowing, and as Stiles sprawled beside it, heaving, Derek sniffed at it for a while, grunted, and added some twigs to make the flames jump to life.

"So?" Stiles finally managed to gasp out. "Was the Alpha here?"

"I can't tell." Derek sounded as if he was embarrassed

and angry in equal measures, which Stiles would have found ironic if he hadn't been too busy wheezing. "But he was definitely at Allison's car."

Stiles closed his eyes against a bombardment of panic. He tried to remind himself that the Alpha had bitten Scott because he needed him. An Alpha derived strength from his pack members. So he wouldn't kill Scott. Allison was another subject. Her father was a werewolf hunter. What if the Alpha attacked her out of revenge?

"I'm going to look for Scott," Derek said.

"Hang on. I'll go with—" Stiles couldn't finish his sentence. He lay gasping. Then he raised a hand. "—you," he said at last.

But Derek was already gone.

"Or I'll just lie here and pass out," Stiles muttered.

"Lydia, there's someone to see you," Lydia's mother told her with a soft rap on her door.

Finally, Lydia thought. She had had enough of plucking her eyebrows and redoing her manicure and reading about the history of Fermat's theorem while awaiting Jackson's return from his rendezvous with Hunter Gramm. She was lying on her bed in China blue tap pants and a camisole and had just enough time to check her lip gloss—and for it to occur to her that that "someone" might be Allison's supersnoopy Aunt Kate—before the door opened, revealing Danny, Jackson's best friend, and a guy Danny'd been hanging out with—Damon somebody.

"Oh," she said, disappointed. She sat up. "Hi."

Dark-haired, with that cool Hawaiian vibe he had, Danny raised his hand in greeting. Damon did the same.

"Is Jackson here?" he asked.

"You could have called to find out that no, he isn't," she scolded him, closing her book and setting it on her night-stand.

"We were driving by anyway. And I don't have your number. And he's not answering his phone."

Don't I know it, she thought.

"Jackson was supposed to meet up for scrimmage this morning," Danny said, "and he promised Damon that he'd burn him a playlist to give the DJ for his birthday party. Which is tomorrow, and we're getting a bit concerned."

Her first impulse was to lie to them both and make up some reason for why Jackson wasn't there, but then it dawned on her that Jackson might have assumed that when he said "home soon" he meant *his* home. *How* could she have lain all alone in her room without that occurring to her? Surely he would have contacted her, though, when he got to his house and she hadn't shown.

But why would he even bother? a little voice whispered in her suspicious ear. *He didn't bother to call you last night, did he?*

"Here's the thing," she blurted, to shut the evil voice up. "I was just about to go over to his house. He got held up on his . . . appointment and so it's . . . time for me to check to make sure everything's fine. Since his parents are gone."

"Like, water the plants?" Damon deadpanned.

"Yes," Lydia huffed. "Jackson loves me to water his plants."

Danny raised a brow. "But where's he been? Why all the mystery?"

"If Jackson wants to share, he'll share," she said, hinting without actually saying it that she knew and he didn't. Lydia knew the power of secrets. That was how she maintained control of her clique at school. You doled out information, letting some people have a little more than others. Teasing outsiders with the possibility of being in the inner sanctum. Excluding them when they misbehaved.

The way you maintained boyfriends, now that she thought of it.

He is so going to regret this stunt, she promised herself.

She slid off the bed and Danny looked even more taken aback.

"What?" she asked.

He gave her a completely nonsexual once-over. "Are you going in that?"

She tossed her hair disdainfully and walked to her closet. Her hand came down on a pair of designer jeans and she passed. She was not a blue jeans kind of girl, especially not tonight, when she was out to remind Jackson what he had been missing and could possibly continue to miss unless he begged for her forgiveness. Going in for the kill, she selected a short gray and berry plaid skirt with a matching cashmere sweater and flounced into her bathroom.

She took her time getting ready—she always made boys wait, even gay ones—and came out looking (she hoped) cool, collected, and not like some desperate girlfriend going in search of her AWOL boyfriend, on what could have been their second night of hookup bliss.

"You look nice," Damon said, and she beamed at him.

"So do you," she said, sliding her coat off its hanger. "You can follow me over," she added. She'd need her car if she was going to stay, which she hadn't decided yet. And if there was any reason to stay.

"Be right back," she said to the guys.

There was the matter of protecting Allison from any more phone calls, of course. She quietly glided into her mother's bedroom and lifted the landline off the hook, placing the handset behind her mother's nightstand, and turning down the ringer so that the incessant buzz wouldn't tip off her mom when she went to bed. Her mother would assume she'd knocked it off herself. She wasn't a suspicious parent, and the fact that she and Lydia's father had gotten divorced made her more lenient than other moms. A lot more lenient that Allison's aunt.

God.

Next Lydia went into the little workout room her mom had put together in the spare room where her dad used to have his home office. That was where she'd put the treadmill. Dressed in tasteful sweats, her mom was striding off the pounds, watching something on the plasma with her earbuds in, and Lydia waved at her.

Ms. Martin pulled out a bud as she kept striding. "Yes, honey?"

"Allison," was all Lydia said.

Her mom frowned slightly, looking a little unclear, but nodded anyway and put her earbud back in.

"Have fun," she said, too loudly, and Lydia hid a little smile. Sometimes, when dealing with parents, less was more.

Now, if Allison's mom, dad, aunt, or some random long-distance friend in San Francisco called, her mom would accidentally fill in whatever blank they offered her. *Why, yes, they did go to the library. Lydia mentioned something about that to me.*

It wasn't a perfect solution, and Lydia very much hoped Allison wouldn't wind up in trouble, but sometimes you had to take risks in this life.

The Whittemores lived in one of the biggest and most expensive houses, if not the most, in Beacon Hills; an estate, really, well away from the street, in an almost countrylike setting. Lydia clicked in the security code and drove on in. Danny and Damon followed in Danny's car.

When they reached the driveway and there was no familiar Porsche there, Lydia's stomach did a little flip. *He texted that he was on his way back.* Sure, the woods were a ways away, but he'd had more than enough time to make the trip twice and still have time to go shopping for a nice piece of jewelry to accessorize his apology.

Still, a girl had her pride, and although she wasn't sure if she should continue to honor Jackson's privacy by not involving Danny, or even, at this point, Sheriff Stilinski, she keyed in the front door code, as well, and opened the door with a flourish.

As Jackson's best friend, Danny had been to his extravagant home before, but the splendor was all new to Damon. Standing beneath the skylight in the living room, he looked at Danny with newfound respect, and Lydia concealed a grin. She was happy to help Danny with his romance, in her own small way.

They went upstairs to Jackson's room and she flicked on the light switch. There, alas, was his empty bed, still rumpled from when she laid waiting for him the night before. She took off her coat and laid it on the bed, then went straight to the drawer where she'd found the note and casually moved some things around—athletic cup, eww—checking to see if she'd missed a vital piece of information about his whereabouts.

"Are you looking through his stuff?" Danny queried, and she gave him her best patronizing look.

"Please," she said. "You must know that I have a drawer here."

Damon looked even more impressed. Very few teenagers could claim the very adult perk of having a drawer containing their belongings at their boy- or girlfriend's house. Not that many teenagers had the need. It spoke of changing clothes, spending the night. Adult stuff.

Sex.

In reality, there was nothing of hers in the drawer, except, oh, *yes.*

She showed them the packet of glow-in-the-dark condoms she had purchased Jackson for last Valentine's Day. He had refused to use them. Tonight he would. She'd make sure of that.

"Have you ever tried these?" she asked, showing them to the guys. Damon guffawed, and Danny grinned. "Want a sample in case you decide to play the home version?"

"Pass," Danny said, and Lydia supposed it would be some

sort of violation of the man code to use your best friend's condoms.

"So where is he?" Damon said, looking around at Jackson's vast collection of sports trophies, plaques, and team photos. "Maybe the CD's around here?"

"Could be," she said, wishing she'd thought of that excuse before she'd pawed around in his drawer. She didn't know why Jackson hadn't just set up a shareable playlist for Damon, but he wasn't here to explain. So she sat at his desk and flipped on his desktop.

His wallpaper was a picture of her—one she had picked out herself, and approved of—and she typed in "CAPTAIN" when prompted for the password that would unlock the secrets of Jackson to her prying eyes.

If he ever did anything like this to me, I would dump him in a heartbeat, she thought. *That's where we're so different.*

She also opened a couple of the desk drawers. No more cryptic envelopes presented themselves.

"He usually keeps playlists in a folder," she lied, running the cursor over Jackson's private affairs. She was beginning to feel like she'd pushed this maneuver about as far as she could with witnesses present. Maybe inviting them over hadn't been her cleverest move. She was beginning to feeling guilty about Allison, too.

"Do you think we're ready for a drawer?" Damon murmured to Danny, and she smiled to herself again.

Then Danny said, "What was that?"

She made a half turn. "What was what?"

"I heard a noise," he said. "It sounded like it was in the garage."

She pictured the automatic garage door opening, Jackson's Porsche gliding in, the door closing. *Yes.*

Smoothing back her hair, she said, "You wait here. I'll let him know we have company."

She turned off the computer and walked from the room. She crossed the distance of the enormous house to the garage, and was about to open the interior door that led to the garage when the knob turned.

"You're in such trouble," she said in a kittenish voice, to take the sting out of her genuine ire.

The door slammed open. Something hit her in the face and threw her to the floor. Stunned, she saw nothing but a huge black shape as she was dragged away. She tried to scream but she was so shocked all she could do was gasp.

"He said no one would be home," a guy said in a low, gravelly voice. He sounded young, maybe early twenties. She blinked her eyes rapidly and looked up—

—into a ski mask and a pair of hazel eyes glaring down at her.

"Parents are in Europe. Bailey's made contact with Jackson," Ski Mask said. He sounded young, too.

"Then who's she?" the gravelly voiced guy demanded.

Suddenly a gun was pointed in Lydia's face. A real gun. A gun that could kill her. She could feel her eyes crossing as she stared at the barrel with the same gut-churning horror as if he were holding a rattlesnake. She didn't know if she was still breathing. She didn't know anything. She could barely remember how to think.

He was wearing Latex gloves. No fingerprints left behind. Nothing left behind, except, possibly, a dead girl.

"You make *one* sound," Ski Mask warned her. "Understand?"

She tried to move her head, but she was paralyzed with fear. He touched the tip of the gun against her forehead. She went completely cold, head to toe, as if someone had just dumped her in a frozen river.

"Understand?"

All she could do was lie there.

"What the *hell* are we going to do with her?" Gravelly Voice said. He came into the room. He, too, was wearing a mask. And Latex gloves.

"Is there anyone else in the house?" Ski Mask asked her. "Tell me the truth or I'll blow you away."

Lydia lay petrified, still unable to speak.

After shedding himself of Stiles, Derek had made the shift and charged through the woods. He stayed well hidden, slinking through a copse of trees as he came within sight of some people partying at a fire ring. They were drinking and laughing, just a bunch of kids messing around, savoring the freedom of a Friday night. The pungent odors of sweat, smoke, and alcohol created a near-impenetrable layer of smells, and he scented no trace of either the Alpha or Scott.

Frustrated, he moved on, loping through the woods. He stayed low, racing along, until he smelled traces of Scott and the Alpha. His hackles rose, and he let out a growl that almost rose into a howl, but at the last instant, he suppressed it. Both sets of traces were old, and hadn't mingled.

At different times, each of them had been there. But neither tonight. Scott might find it bitterly ironic to know that he had crossed the Alpha's path before the Alpha had changed his life forever.

And then Derek touched down on the spot where he had found his sister's body. In fury, he showed his teeth and threw back his head, forcing down another howl, this one of rage. He bit down on his arm to stop himself, almost welcoming the deep pain he felt.

As the wound began to heal, he moved on, searching for Scott, following another smoke trail until he came to another fire. This one was unattended. He smelled humans very clearly. There had been two. One, he didn't recognize, but the other was that surly lacrosse player, the one he'd dug his nails into when he'd been so sick and the kid had been so insulting.

Jackson.

In his anger, Derek shifted back to human form. He'd been dying of wolfsbane poisoning when he'd lashed out at Jackson, grabbing him by the back of the neck. He hadn't meant to dig his nails into him. But now Jackson bore Derek's mark, and the Alpha would know him by it. It had been such a stupid thing to do.

I couldn't help it, he reminded himself as he walked the perimeter of the fire. He didn't like the smell of the other man who had been there with Jackson. Jackson had been afraid of him. Derek could smell it.

There was something half burned in the fire, what looked like a photocopy of a newspaper article. Derek fished it out. It bore the smell of the stranger:

JACKSON WHITTEMORE BREAKS HIGH SCHOOL
STATE RECORD FOR POINTS PER GAME.

Jackson Whittemore, captain of the Beacon Hills boys lacrosse team, continues to astonish with a 17 percent increase
in his goals per games stats over last year

Most of the rest of the article was burned, which was fine
with Derek, because it was boring. He was about to toss it
back into the fire when he idly turned it over. There was
what appeared to be an address, followed by a string of let-
ters and numbers. It looked like some kind of code. Shrug-
ging, he folded it up and stuck it into his jacket pocket.
It might come in handy. He was keeping tabs on Jackson
Whittemore.

He kicked dirt into the fire to put it out, at the same
time digging around with a stick for more souvenirs from
Jackson's encounter with the young man, finding nothing.
As the earth smothered the fire, he smelled more smoke.

This is getting ridiculous, he thought. He was beginning to
suspect someone was deliberately setting fires to throw him
off the scent. Images from his dream tumbled through his
mind, and he raced back into the darkness.

CHAPTER ELEVEN

Stiles was seriously beginning to lose it. He was scared, and cold, and worried about Scott and Allison. He'd even stumbled back to Allison's car and then returned to where Derek dumped him, as terrified as he was about running into the Alpha. Somehow he'd hoped he would find something that would tell him where they were.

He sat on a log, tossing twigs and leaves into the fire, which really didn't help it grow. There was an art to these things, he knew. He'd actually been a Cub Scout, but he'd been booted for being too talkative during meetings. Go figure.

He tried calling Scott a couple more times, then Allison, then Lydia. He'd had her phone in his possession when he'd deleted the picture she'd accidentally taken of the Alpha. Of course he'd also inputted her number into his own phone; how stalkerish was that?

Taking a breath, he dialed the divine Ms. Martin, and waited. He had a queasy moment imagining Jackson, with

Lydia, answering his call instead of her. Stiles nearly hung up, but he waited until it went to voice.

"Hey, just checking in on our boy," he said, hoping that was sufficiently vague. Then he sighed and hung up, and thought about playing Angry Birds or something to pass the time.

"I couldn't find them," Derek said, coming up behind him, and Stiles let out a shriek.

"Can you not do that?" he said. "You're going to give me a heart attack."

Derek sat down on the log beside him. He was kind of sweaty, and he looked glummer than usual. Stiles drummed his fingers on the log, waiting for Derek to bring him up to date.

Finally, he couldn't take the silence any longer and said, "So?"

"There are fires all over the forest," Derek said. "I think the Alpha has been setting them so I wouldn't be able to smell Scott."

Stiles crossed his arms and hunched over, shivering and trying to make himself inconspicuous, in case the Alpha spotted Derek and decided to attack him. But Derek was a Beta werewolf, too, like Scott. Why wasn't he part of the Alpha's pack?

Maybe he is. Maybe he just hasn't told us, he thought.

"Or maybe it's some kind of trap," Derek said. "Something the Argents cooked up."

"You mean that Allison's in on it?" Stiles asked, sounding incredulous.

Derek slid a glance at him. "Why do you sound so surprised? You know what the Argents are. What they do."

"But Allison's different," Stiles said. "She's totally into Scott. She'd never do anything to hurt him."

"We can't trust human women," Derek replied. "Believe me, I know." He stared into the flames, and remembered.

Beacon Hills
Six Years Earlier

Derek swam.

Lap after lap, after school, he did laps to burn off the extra testosterone. On Mondays, he would begin the school week, wedged in with all the humans, watching their power plays, sometimes mixing it up with them, getting flirted with and hit on by girls he knew he should avoid. He stayed on alert all week, until by Friday, he thought he would explode from the pressure.

Added to that, Wolf Moon was coming in a month. Hales from all over the country would be arriving for the big ritual, when they honored their ancestor, the Beast of Gévaudan, the one who, it was said, created their werewolf heritage. Derek was sixteen, the age of manhood in their pack, and he would be taking his place among the adult males. His cousin Josh would be there, and Derek was anticipating his challenge for rank in the hierarchy. Josh was sixteen, too. And so Derek swam, for endurance, and lifted weights, for strength, and told himself over and over that he had just as good a chance at winning the challenge as Josh did.

Derek wanted to see his father collect on the bet he'd made with Uncle Peter. His dad was betting on Derek;

Uncle Peter favored Josh, who was his sister-in-law's kid. Derek's sister, Laura, had told him that the two senior Hale males were keeping statistics on Derek and Josh—height, weight, workout regimes. Derek was insulted. Of *course* he could best his cousin.

Laura thought it was all so funny. That afternoon, in the cafeteria, she had mocked his supershake, the drink he had concocted that included ginseng energy boosts he bought from a senior named Michael Foy, whose father was into Chinese medicine.

"Josh is two inches taller than you," she'd reminded him. "You can't take anything that will make you taller."

"Less than one inch," Derek corrected her. "And he moves like a lumber truck."

Swim it off. Grow strong, he told himself, as his hands sliced through the water.

One by one, the other swimmers finished their routines and got out. They had dates, and friends. Movies and parties to go to. Derek stayed aloof. Unlike Laura, who was popular, he didn't have any human friends, and he didn't want any.

Swim it off. Grow strong.

"Derek," said Mr. Braswell, the basketball coach who also served as the after-school lifeguard. He was standing at the edge of the pool. "Remember, I'm taking some personal time while my wife's home on maternity. My substitute starts on Monday. I've been looking the other way and letting you stay in the pool after hours, but you should probably play it cool. He probably won't go for it."

"Yeah, okay," Derek said, frustrated. He didn't see why he couldn't sign a form or something saying that he was assuming the risk of swimming without a lifeguard. Swimming got it done for him the way nothing else did. He wanted to be ready for the challenge.

He wanted Uncle Peter to lose that bet.

The following Monday, after the final bell, Derek suited up in the locker room, putting on his black Speedo and showering before he hit the pool. With his towel over his shoulders, he warmed up a little, making circles with his neck and rolling his shoulders as he observed the other lap swimmers. The swim coach kept begging Derek to join the team, but Derek and his father both agreed that would be taking too many chances. It was difficult enough controlling himself at school, and the swim team traveled to meets. How would he explain his refusal to participate on trips taking place during the full moon?

He was about to dive into the water when he remembered that there was a new lifeguard. He looked across at the lifeguard tower, and he nearly fell in. The sub was a young woman—the most beautiful girl he had ever seen in his life. Her body was more sinewy than most swimmers', and her black suit was definitely not regulation. Her honey-brown hair was shoulder length and her eyes were green, like a mermaid's.

Don't wolf, he told himself. *Stay calm.*

She smiled straight at him, leaning forward in that amazing, clinging Spandex suit of hers. He looked away, and his enhanced hearing picked up her lusty chuckle. Fighting to retain command of himself, he dove in from the side of the pool—not the best of swim manners, since he nearly collided with a girl who was doing the backstroke in the lane he dove into.

"Hey!" the girl cried, flailing as Derek came up for air. She waved her hand at the lifeguard. "Ms. Argent! Did you see that?"

The lifeguard—Ms. Argent—climbed down from her perch and sauntered over to the side of the pool. Derek slicked back his hair and ducked under the nylon lane line, meeting her there.

"You're Derek Hale," she said.

"Yes." He couldn't keep his eyes off her legs. They were amazing, muscular and long, and her suit bottom rode high on her hipbones. "Sorry about that."

"You shouldn't be sorry," she said with a little smile, gaze traveling from his face to the waterline and back again. "Being Derek Hale looks pretty good to me."

He felt himself go hot. It was a good thing he was in the pool.

"Mr. Braswell said you like to swim late," she said. "I'm cool with that."

"I'll lock up," he promised.

"That won't be necessary," she said. Her eyes were so incredibly green, and her coy little smile made his stomach dance. He was riveted.

Then she turned around and sauntered back toward the tower. Derek watched her, his predatory instincts coming into play.

She's human, he reminded himself, but he couldn't stop looking at her. He followed her every move as she climbed back onto her tower and laid the mandated rescue float across her lap. She was catlike, lithe and strong, and he was mesmerized. She knew it, too, judging by the way she gave her hair a toss and smiled at him again.

Swim it off, he ordered himself, finding an empty lane and putting on his swim goggles. Then he moved his shoulders and neck to work out the brand-new kinks, and began to swim. He didn't follow any kind of program. He just did lap after lap.

Then he became aware of someone swimming in his lane. That happened; when the pool was crowded, swimmers shared lanes, one swimming from shallow to deep, and the other going from deep to shallow. As he raised his arm and took a breath, he caught a flash of honey-brown hair and green eyes. Then, through the water, a musky scent traveled toward him.

Kate Argent was in the pool, sharing his lane. He jerked, losing his rhythm, and stopped swimming. They were alone in the water, just the two of them. All the other lanes were empty.

She's coming on to me, he thought. He couldn't believe it.

She kept going, passing him by, and he watched her, stunned and unsure. When she reached the wall, she did a flip-kick and headed back. Would anything happen when she reached him?

He thought about reaching out, touching her. He wanted to, with all his straining body. But she was practically a teacher, and he was only sixteen. Of course she was just toying with him. She probably had a boyfriend or a husband waiting for her.

Flustered, even a little frightened, Derek ducked beneath the nylon lane divider, reached the side, and climbed out of the pool. He left without saying a word, heading for the boys' locker room. Her amused laughter trailed after him.

He was almost afraid to shower, but he quickly rinsed off and changed into street clothes, still mostly wet. He practically ran out of the school, looking over his shoulder.

She was standing in the parking lot, scanning the cars. Moonlight gleamed on her hair, which was slicked away from her face. She was wearing a black V-neck sweater, tight jeans, and heeled boots that clung to her calves. His vision wolfed, and he turned his head away quickly before the telltale glow revealed his secret—although it was likely she'd assume the headlights from the cars on the road were being reflected in his eyes.

Her body was so curvaceous, and her features were so pretty. He wanted to growl to her, speak of his desire for her, but he pushed it all away and loped down the street.

He was due to meet his sister at the Beaconburger, a local hangout. Involved in school with friends, Laura was always content to wait for him so they could drive home together. They shared a Subaru Forester, not the coolest car, but Derek was planning to get something of his own once he landed a part-time job. Their dad said he could start looking if he kept his grades up. Derek was smart, and his GPA showed it. Laura, too.

He looked through the window at his sister. Laura was sitting in a maroon pleather booth reading a book. A Diet Coke and a very rare hamburger were placed before her. Brother and sister had started eating occasionally at the

Beaconburger before they went home after school. It helped cut down on the traffic in the kitchen as their mom began preparations for Wolf Moon.

He went inside, and she raised her chin the merest fraction of an inch, scenting him.

Hey," she said, smiling as he approached. Then something must have shown on his face, because her smile faded and she put her book aside. "Derek? Are you okay?"

He looked hard at her. Then he shook his head. "I'm not," he told her.

She gestured to the empty seat across the table. He sat down very slowly, almost as if he couldn't remember how to make his human body move. He felt strangely weightless.

She pushed the hamburger at him. "You look kind of pale. Did you overdo it in the pool?"

"There was this girl. Woman," he said. He licked his lips. "Laura, she was . . . she's beautiful." He shook his head, dumbfounded. "She's so beautiful."

Laura blinked at him. Then she grinned. "Could she be . . . beautiful?"

He pursed his lips and took a drink from her Diet Coke.

"Is this . . . woman a student?" Laura asked.

"No. She's the new lifeguard. Ms. Argent. Mr. Braswell's replacement."

"*School* lifeguard?" she said, looking mildly shocked. "A teacher?"

"I know." He ran a hand through his hair. It was still wet, and he looked down at his hand as if seeing it for the first time. "She went swimming with me. Laps. I was alone in the water and then she was there." He saw her sleek body moving through the water. Remembered her scent, and her husky laugh.

"It was like swimming with a wild thing," he said.

"Oh?" Laura cocked her head and sat back in the booth. "And . . . did you *do* the wild thing?"

"What?" He jerked back to reality. To the booth, and the noisy crowd, and his sister, practically laughing out loud at him. "No!"

"Don't look so insulted," she said. "You're sixteen, Derek. In our world . . . matable."

"Sh," he cautioned her. "Not so loud. Someone might hear."

She made a *pfft* sound. "Don't worry. I can barely hear myself in this din." Still, she leaned toward him, grinning and peering up at him through her lashes. "So . . . she came onto you like a big slut?"

He blushed. Suddenly he didn't feel like talking to her about it anymore. It felt like he was saying bad things about Ms. Argent, but he couldn't really explain why. Because they were packmates, he and Laura were relatively close as teenage brothers and sisters went, but on occasion he'd gotten weary listening to her chatter on about her crushes on human boys and dissect each thing her girlfriends said and what they wore and who they went out with. But now the tables were turned, kind of. And he wasn't used to talking about himself, and everything in him was denying that Ms. Argent had done anything *slutty*.

He picked the bun off her hamburger, staring down at the bloody meat, and replaced the bun.

"She's not really a teacher," he said. "She's just a life-guard."

She gestured to the hamburger. "Go ahead. Eat."

"I'm not hungry," he said.

She leaned forward on her hands and giggled at her so-very-serious little brother.

"Then maybe you're in love. *Puppy* love," she added, giggling some more.

A few booths down, Scott McCall put down the cheeseburger from his kiddie meal. "I'm not hungry," he said miserably. He wanted to get away from the arguing. His parents always fought a lot, but today it was worse. Something had happened. Something bad. "Can I have money for video games?"

"No," his father snapped, as his mom opened her purse. "We don't have enough money for crap like that. Am I right, Melissa?"

"I have a couple of quarters," Scott's mom said, ignoring his father. And somehow, even though he was only ten years old, he knew it would be better to take them than to explain to her that there was only one game in the entire Beaconburger that took less than a dollar. And that it was a stupid game, and he didn't like to play it.

He held out his hand for her to drop the quarters in, but his dad clamped his fingers around Scott's wrist. It hurt, but he pretended that it didn't as he watched his mom looking through her purse.

Then Scott felt his chest go tight, and a crackle of distress snapped through him. It was starting. He was going to have an asthma attack. Here. Now.

In front of his father.

"I'm getting mixed messages," his father said to his mom, who looked up from her purse and saw that his dad had hold of Scott's wrist. "First we don't have enough money to pay for cable. But we have enough money for Scott's inhaler. We don't have enough money for a down payment on a new car but we can stop in here at the Beaconburger instead of eating at home, where mac and cheese is a dollar a box."

"Let go of my son," his mom said in a low, deadly voice. Then, very softly, "Scott, do you need your inhaler?"

Scott pursed his lips together. He was trying to push the air down his windpipe into his lungs. Each puff of the inhaler cost money. His dad always said so. He didn't want his dad to get madder. Scott didn't want him to yell at his mom because Scott had asthma. It wasn't her fault. It was his, Scott's.

"Hold on, Scott," she said, reaching back into her purse. "I've got it right here."

"He doesn't need that," Scott's father said. "It's all in his head."

Scott pushed harder, but it wasn't working. He began to wheeze.

"Let go of him," his mom said again. "Scott, here." She held out the inhaler.

His father kept a painful grip on Scott's wrist, grinding the bones together. Tears welled in Scott's eyes as he gazed at his lifesaver—the inhaler.

"You baby him. That's why he thinks he's so delicate. C'mon, Scott." His dad jiggled his wrist. "Stop being such a wimp."

There was no air in his lungs. None in his body. He couldn't get any. His mom's eyes got big, and she turned the full force of her gaze on his dad.

"Let go of my son, *now*," she said. "Let go of him or I swear to God, I will deck you."

No, I'll breathe, Scott promised her, promised them, if only to make it all stop. But he couldn't. He was beginning to see yellow and gray dots.

His mom half rose out of her chair. Scott's father made a show of releasing Scott, and Scott grabbed the inhaler from his mom and took a puff. His air passages opened and he sucked in air. He took another puff, even though each puff cost money, and shut his eyes as he trembled with relief.

"Yeah, he's your son, all right," Scott's father said. "But maybe he's not mine."

Her eyes narrowed. She hated his dad. Anyone could see that. "Scott, are you all right?" she asked him.

No, he wanted to tell her. *I'm not. And I won't be, ever. Not as long as he's with us.*

"We need to go home. He needs to rest," she said.

His father grabbed his mom's purse and yanked out her wallet. His hand shook as he handed Scott a five-dollar bill.

"Go play your damned video games," he hissed at him.

Scott took the money and stumbled away. Passing table after table, he heard some girl talking to some boy about being in love.

I will never fall in love, Scott vowed. *Ever.*

CHAPTER TWELVE

Beacon Hills Preserve
The Present

As Scott cuddled Allison against the chill, he sighed. He didn't want to move on, but each minute that they spent making out, they weren't looking for her keys.

"Allison, we should look some more," he said, and she kissed him again.

"I know. This is just . . . so nice."

They both got to their feet. They were only about two-thirds of the way along the original path they had first taken, walking beside a steep incline that shot down into the darkness. There was still hope that they could find her keys.

"Don't worry, we'll find them," he said, and he squeezed her hand. She smiled gamely at him.

Then her phone rang. Her brows shot up and she reached into the pocket of her heavy coat. But as she pulled her hand back out, she stumbled backward and let go of the phone.

"Whoops," she said.

"I'll get it," he said, but she was already pivoting around to retrieve it.

Her momentum carried her forward, and, to Scott's shock, she began sliding down the incline. Her feet shot out from beneath her as she accelerated.

"Allison!" he cried, reaching out to stop her.

He grabbed her hand, but her weight yanked him off balance and he crashed to the ground. Then the incline angled down more sharply, practically perpendicular, and they began falling nearly headlong into darkness.

Scott tried to latch on to branches as they plummeted, fighting to hold onto Allison, but her fingers slid out of his grasp and he heard her cry out. Rocks pelted his face and body, and his shoulder slammed hard against a boulder. He tried to catch hold of it but no luck.

"Allison!" he yelled.

There was no answer as the rocks rolled around him and he kept sliding down.

He felt himself begin to wolf and realized that if he let himself do it, he could at least see where she was falling.

No, stop, he ordered himself.

"Allison!" he called again.

Nothing.

If she saw him turn, so much would go wrong. But he had to chance it. He tried to limit it to eyesight only, and scarlet infrared bathed the tumbling world around him. He still didn't see Allison anywhere.

Let her be okay, let her be okay, he pleaded as he fell. He kept trying to grab onto something, anything. The skin on his hands was being sliced; everything stung.

Then he landed hard on spongy earth and lay panting. Fear whooshed up and around him like waves. He made himself hide the wolf away and sprawled on the ground, hurting everywhere.

"Scott?" Allison said hoarsely. "Scott!"

"I'm here," he said, reaching out his arms, trying to find her without his enhanced vision. Their hands met, and he pulled Allison into his very-human embrace.

"Are you okay?" she asked. She covered his face with quick kisses. "Are you all right?"

"I'm fine. What about you?" He had werewolf healing powers. She didn't. He touched her face. There was a scratch on her cheek, and leaves in her hair, but she looked relatively unscathed.

"I'm okay." He picked some of the leaves out of her hair. "I got some scrapes on my legs but it's nothing major."

"I'm glad," he said, and kissed her. "Hey, Allison," he whispered in her ear. "I'm falling for you. Head over heels."

She snickered. "Nice one," she said. Then she picked a leaf off his arm, like they were two animals grooming each other. "Do you think we're being punished for sneaking out when we're grounded?"

"No. I think we'll be punished if we're caught," he replied, grinning at her.

"Then let's make a pact that we won't be caught," she said. She sat up very straight and held up her right hand. "I, Allison Argent, do solemnly swear *not* to get busted by my parents."

"And I, Scott McCall, solemnly swear that, too." He threaded his fingers through hers. She smiled at him.

And then she made her "uh-oh" face.

"I think I lost my phone." She groaned. "My keys *and* my phone."

"Maybe it fell down with us," he suggested. "Unless it can defy gravity."

"Or it got stuck on something," she said uneasily. "I swear, Scott, are we in a Roadrunner cartoon?"

"Only if an anvil falls on our heads. Yikes, duck!" he cried, throwing his hands over his head.

She smiled gamely and gave him a teasing swat on his arm, but he could feel her dismay. Grinning, he looked downward and let his eyesight shift. This felt like a math problem, not his strong suit, but he was willing to give it a shot: if he were falling a hundred miles an hour down a twenty-thousand-foot drop, at a velocity of whatever, and he were a phone, where would he land?

Right there!

Her phone was a small red rectangle about ten feet away from them, lodged among dozens, if not hundreds, of tall, spindly bushes with white flowers and clumps of red berries.

It was too dark for him to have reasonably spotted it in normal life, so he kept pretending to inspect the ground. Allison was right beside him, glancing up and around.

"We can use my phone to call it," Scott suggested, pulling out his phone. His charge was at 9 percent. "Let's make this count. My battery is super low."

She nodded and held her breath while he pressed in her number. Her phone trilled in the bushes. Her ringtone for him was Kids of 88. Nice.

"Yes!" she cried, hugging him. They both darted toward the bushes. Scott lunged for the phone, reaching out . . . and found he couldn't seem to move his hand forward.

"What?" he said. "Allison?"

She darted past him and stared at the wall of greenery. "I don't see it," she said. "Call again, please."

He was staring straight at it. It was about three layers of branches in. But as he put his hand forward, it was as if he touched some kind of invisible barrier.

What the heck?

"There," he said, pointing. "See it?"

"Yes!" she cried. She pushed herself into the mass of leaves and branches and snagged her phone. "Yes, yes, yes!"

She whirled around and fought her way back through. Dancing a little, she hugged him. He soaked it up and hugged her back.

Then she pulled away so she could look at him. "Why couldn't you get it?" she asked him. "Are you hurt?"

Now what do I say? he thought, studying the bushes. Were they some kind of wolfsbane? He tried again to move into them. It was exactly as if a force field prevented him.

She was waiting for his answer. Maybe he could pretend to be scared or have some kind of weird phobia.

About touching bushes?

"Um, yeah," he said. He faked a limp forward, and then he sank to the ground. "Something's wrong with my leg. I didn't notice at first because . . . because of the adrenaline. But it's hurting a lot." He hated lying to her.

"Oh, no," she said, falling down beside him. "Do you think you broke something?"

"No." He didn't want to upset her. "Just, um, a sprain. I'm sure it'll be better soon. If I just rest a minute."

"Okay." She sat down beside him. "Wow, I totally didn't notice that hill." She laid her head on her knees and grinned weakly over at him. "But I was a little distracted."

"Me, too. Are you okay?" he asked worriedly. She seemed okay.

"I'm fine," she insisted. "But I'm worried about you. If you can't walk, how are we going to get out of here?"

"You can carry me," he suggested.

"Right."

"Sure. Over your shoulder. You could totally do it."

"Well, I'd need a machete to cut down all those bushes first," she said, laughing. "But once you're feeling up to it—*if* you're feeling up to it—we might be able to work our way through them."

"Sure," he said, realizing he was going to have to make sure he didn't feel up to it. Unless he could figure why he couldn't do it now. There was so much about being a werewolf that he didn't know. Okay, he hardly knew anything. If Derek were here . . .

Derek, he thought. *I can text him and ask him*. But Derek didn't have a cell phone. *Argh, Derek. You complicate my life on so many levels.*

"All this to find Jackson," Allison muttered. "He'd better be awfully grateful."

"Yeah," he said noncommittally. He wondered if going through all this for the sake of a guy who didn't like him marked him as an idiot, or a wuss, or worse.

"This was so nice of you," she went on. "Think what

would have happened if Lydia and I had come out here, and my aunt had called her house. If she hadn't been there to answer the landline . . ." She mimicked slicing her throat.

He cocked his head. "What would have happened?"

She moved her shoulders, and her features darkened. "I don't actually know. I've always been pretty close to my folks, you know? Because we move so much. This is the first time I've really had friends . . . or a boyfriend." She wrinkled her nose at him as if testing out the word.

"We're very friendly here in Beacon Hills," he told her, grinning back at her. *Loving* hearing the word *boyfriend* on her lips, referring to him. Then he bent over and kissed her, and she slid her arms around his neck.

"So I see. But anyway, to answer your question, this is a new subject for my family and me. Me being in trouble. And . . . us not being as close," she added faintly. She frowned and got a faraway look on her face. "Things are . . . different."

Don't I know it. He was used to keeping things from his mom, though. He didn't like to worry her, and it felt weird going to her with questions about . . . well, anything. He and Stiles had kind of raised each other.

"Lydia and Jackson are probably making up," she murmured.

"Making out," he said, and lowered his head toward her.

"Wait. How's your ankle?" she asked him.

"It doesn't matter. I don't kiss with my ankle." He tried to remember if he'd actually said that it was his ankle that was bothering him. He didn't know what to do.

"I'm sure it'll get better in a few minutes," he said. "It's just in shock." He made a look of mock concern. "I hope it doesn't sue me."

Her smile didn't reach past her eyes. She was worried about him. That was so *cool*.

"Maybe I could look at it," she said. She moved her shoulder. "I don't know first aid, but you do. You made a splint for that dog I hit. You could tell me what to do." She gestured to the bushes. "We have plenty of wood to make a splint."

His mind was racing. He wondered what would happen if he had her make a splint from one of the bushes. Maybe it would work like when Derek had burned the Northern Blue Monkshood and then pushed it into the bullet hole in his arm. Used the poison to cure the poison. But were the bushes *poison*?

He looked over his shoulder at the hill they'd just fallen down. *Hill* was definitely the wrong term. It was a freakin' cliff, rising nearly straight up. Grateful Allison hadn't gotten severely injured, he doubted they'd be able to get back up it without rock-climbing equipment.

"Let's make sure your phone works," he said, partly to distract her. "Why don't you check in with Lydia?"

As she nodded and initiated the call, he shifted his vision and scanned the area around them. To his consternation, he realized that the bushes were growing in a semicircle around the cliff, with no breaks. There were only two ways to get out—up the cliff, or through the bushes.

"Call failed," she reported. "But we might get better reception somewhere else." She looked at the bushes. "That stuff is so thick," she murmured. Then she looked back at him. "Are you feeling any better?"

"Worse," he said, lying. He needed some time to figure out what to do. They were scared, but Allison wasn't hurt. They weren't in imminent danger of getting found out, and except for the intense fear factor, being here with her was pretty sweet.

He handed her his phone. "We don't have a lot of chances to call on my cell," he reminded her. "We have to make them count. I've got the reception but you've got the power. Maybe we should try texting somebody. I'll try Stiles."

"Okay." She nodded. She leaned over his shoulder and he realized that he wouldn't be able to tell Stiles everything. He'd have to try to speak in code. So he wrote: *We r stuck here, bottom of cliff.* Then he took a picture of the bushes and attached it to his text. As an afterthought he snapped a picture of the cliff and sent that as well. *Then* he realized he had Where's My Phone on his phone, too, and of course Stiles knew his user name and password: *Allison* and *Allison.* If his battery didn't die, and Stiles got the texts, he'd realize where they were, and see that they were in trouble.

Hunter Gramm really did have a gun.

But Jackson Whittemore was not about to become a victim.

There was no way Gramm was going to fire a weapon out in the open. There might not be anyone in the lot itself, but there were other people in the preserve, and someone was bound to hear.

Cassie, he thought. Then, *Wait.* His mind racing, he reviewed their conversations. Could she have been in on it? Luring him here for this guy?

Right now, that didn't matter.

He took off running toward his car, yanking out his keys as he did so. His heart was pumping and his mind was racing. *Get to the car, get to the car.* His body, used to sprinting, sucked up the adrenaline and he put on the turbo. His brain, used to defining and achieving goals, spun game plays of him peeling out in the Porsche and calling the police.

Footfalls clattered on the blacktop behind him. Gramm hadn't shot at him, just like he'd expected.

There it was, his Porsche. He got ready to jump in—

—just as another guy in a ski mask popped up from behind it like a jack-in-the-box. He, too, was brandishing a gun.

"Stop right there," he ordered Jackson.

Jackson still would have run, or fought, or yelled, or something, except that Gramm had caught up with him and pressed a gun into his back.

"There's a silencer on this thing," Gramm told Jackson. "Like on TV, you know what I'm talking about? And I won't hesitate to use it."

The other guy came from around the Porsche. He moved swiftly, glancing toward the preserve, aiming his gun at Jackson the entire time. Masked.

"Good timing," Gramm said to the second guy. To Jackson, he said, "Let's go."

Jackson bolted. The second guy ran forward and hit him in the face with something hard. Already exhausted before he'd tried to escape, Jackson lost his footing and went down on one knee. Then he looked up at the two masked guys as they trained their weapons down on him.

"We don't want to hurt you," Gramm said. "Now open your mouth."

Jackson glowered at them both. He was feeling woozy, but he still fought as the other guy stuffed a rag into his mouth, then tied it in place with another rag.

"Hands behind your back," Gramm said.

If I do that I'm a dead man, Jackson thought, not moving a muscle.

The second guy grunted and grabbed one of his arms. Jackson felt something tight clamp around his wrist. Handcuffs. Then the guy pushed his other arm behind Jackson's back and put on the handcuff. When they snapped in place with a click, Jackson flashed with panic.

Someone will come, he told himself. *This is a public place.*

Then something hard came down on the back of his head, and everything went black.

CHAPTER THIRTEEN

Beacon Hills
Six Years Ago

It was Friday, Ms. Argent's fifth day on the job, and after the first day—when she had swum beside him—Derek had caught himself waiting for her to do it again. But she hadn't moved from the lifeguard perch all week, hadn't even spoken to him. She'd just watched him like a hawk, gaze trained on him, as he'd stroked through the water. One by one the other swimmers had left, and he'd remained behind, torn between disappointment that she hadn't done it again, and complete and utter relief that she was staying away from him.

He told himself that he was swimming as long as he always did because the Wolf Moon was coming, and Josh would be training right now, too, getting ready for the challenge. He knew humans had their power plays inside families, but they were nothing compared to those of a werewolf pack. Privileges and status revolved around successful challenges.

As well as around failures.

He swam lap after lap beneath her scrutiny. Then, just as he did one last flip-kick and headed for the stairs in the shallow end, he felt the vibration of her approach in the water.

And then she was swimming alongside him. He couldn't believe it. He didn't know what else to do except to keep swimming. What was he supposed to do? She was probably used to really cool guys. He spun a fantasy of her life before she'd moved to Beacon Hills: living in a big mansion in Sacramento, maybe, or a wicked cool condo. Maybe she'd been an Olympic swimmer and gotten injured or something tragic. He thought about all those human, adult things that he hadn't done, that she obviously had—get a job, have a car. Just . . . leave.

I can't do that, he thought. *I have my pack.*

He'd always been taught that being a werewolf was a gift. Not everyone in his family was so lucky. He had nieces and a couple of cousins who were ordinary; and his old great-uncle was completely human and had never consented to the Bite. What would Ms. Argent think if she knew? Would she think it was cool, or would she turn away from him in horror?

It doesn't matter, he thought. *I can't tell her.*

They swam together, synchronized, and when they hit the five-foot mark, she took his hand and put her feet on the bottom. He stopped, too.

They faced each other.

And she smiled at him, much more shyly than he would have expected. She looked down, then peered up at him through her lashes.

"What you must think of me," she murmured.

His heart was pounding so hard he was sure that she could hear it. He had no idea what to say her, and he also had no idea how to get out of the pool without embarrassing himself.

Except . . . he didn't want to get out of the pool. He wanted to kiss her.

"There's something about you," she whispered. "I've been thinking about you all week. I tried to stay away. I mean, you're a student and I'm . . . well, I'm not a teacher. But I'm close. To being a teacher."

She swirled her fingers in the water. "And this isn't really my style, you know? I don't come on to men like this."

Men. She thought of him as a man. He licked his lips, completely tongue-tied.

"I wish you'd say something," she murmured. "I'm kind of dying about now. I'm sorry if I misread your intentions. I won't bother you again."

His intentions? Misread them? He was baffled. But then he thought about all the looks he had thrown her way. How he'd glanced up at the lifeguard tower every time he'd made a turn to head down the lane. Maybe he had been sending out signals.

"I—I don't want you to get in trouble," he blurted, then flushed because that sounded so wimpy.

Her smile was so sweet. "I don't want to get you in trouble, either," she said. "With the school administration *or* your girlfriend . . ." She trailed off.

"I don't have a girlfriend," he said.

Her cheeks went pink and she smiled, gazing down again. "Oh. I just assumed . . . you being so handsome and all."

His knees almost buckled. He didn't date girls. He had cultivated his status as a loner on purpose, because it made his life easier. But now, facing her, nothing in him wanted to be alone. Sure, Laura's friends flirted with him and told her to tell him that they thought he was hot. But they were girls. Ms. Argent was a *woman*.

"Look," she said. "I— This is happening in such an awkward way. I don't mean to crowd you. I'm just . . . well, I'm drawn to you, and I can't really explain it." She smoothed her wet hair away from her face, and he found the gesture very sexy. "But I don't want you to think I'm just after . . . well, *you* know."

"I—okay," he stammered. "So, um . . . what . . . . ?"

"Do you want to go for coffee?" she asked. He was aware that she was still holding his hand. She caught her breath and let go of it, crossing her arms over her chest. "We could just talk," she suggested. "I'm new here and maybe you could just show me around a little." She raised her brows, looking hopeful and uncertain. I know we'd have to be careful. Outsiders might not understand."

"Yeah," he said. What he didn't know how to explain to her was that he had never taken a girl anywhere in Beacon Hills. He wasn't even sure where to go for coffee. They couldn't go to the Beaconburger—it was far too public— and that was pretty much the only place he knew of that even served coffee.

"I think we're both having the same thought," she murmured. "Privacy."

Privacy, as in being careful not to be seen together while

they were hanging out? Or privacy as in . . . oh, God, was she serious?

"So we can get to know each other." She pondered a moment. "Would you think I was too forward if I invited you to my apartment? Just for coffee?"

"When?" he blurted.

She smiled. "Now?"

His mind was racing so fast it was practically starved for oxygen. He checked the time on the large wall clock. Laura and he were due to meet at the Beaconburger in forty-five minutes. Depending on how far away her apartment was, they could dress quickly, drive over there, chat for a few minutes . . . but there just wasn't enough time.

What if she didn't ask again? He couldn't say no. But he didn't want to say that he had to get a ride home with his sister.

"We only have one car in my family," he said. That wasn't true, but she didn't have to know it.

"I could drive you home."

She looked so hopeful that he almost said yes. But with Wolf Moon approaching, members of the pack would be showing up. He wasn't sure when, but the rules of hospitality always applied—all pack members had a standing invitation to stay at each other's houses.

"I'll just drop you off," she said. "No one will see us."

He was so torn. He wanted to say yes like anything. But he couldn't put his pack in jeopardy by inviting a stranger onto their land. At any other time, he would be able to pull it off. Laura had had friends over, even for overnights on non-full-moon nights. But right now it was too risky.

Talk about horrible timing.

"Another time, then," she said sadly.

"Wait. Let me call my sister," he blurted. And then he was embarrassed because that sounded as if he had to check in with her.

"Laura Hale?" she asked, and he was startled. She blushed again. "I made discreet inquiries about you. Your sister's a senior."

"Yes. Please, wait just a second," he said.

"Okay." She was so sweet.

As he kicked off toward the edge of the pool, he forced himself to slow down. He could swim faster than anyone on the varsity team, but no one could ever know that. Then, as he plodded through the water, he could feel himself begin to wolf. He was too excited. He had to calm down. But how could a sixteen-year-old guy calm down when a beautiful woman like Ms. Argent wanted to get to know him?

Stop, stop, he ordered himself.

He made himself stay in the water until he was sure the wolf shift had reversed itself, and then he scrambled out of the pool. He didn't look back at her as he walked into the boys' locker room. He knew that would look wimpy, and he wanted to be 100 percent positive that there were no telltale signs of the shift on his face—no sprouted hair, no long teeth, no glowing eyes.

Once in the bathroom, he checked his eyes, then opened his locker and got his phone. He called Laura.

"Hey," she said. "Zup?"

"Can you pick me up in three hours?" he asked. He had

no idea where. "At the Beaconburger?" He could always call her back later with a different place. If she said yes.

Say yes, say yes, say yes, Derek silently pleaded.

"What's in it for me?" she asked.

"I won't tell Dad that you were frenching Josh last Wolf Moon."

"I was *not,*" she said indignantly. "I would *never—*"

"And that I have the picture on my phone to prove it," he added smoothly, although he was lying. He didn't have a picture. He even wasn't sure she had been frenching him. But when he'd walked in to call them to the ritual, both of them had messed-up hair and Laura's lipstick was gone. And her lips looked like they'd practically been chewed off.

"Derek," she said. "You *didn't.*"

Ah-ha, and you did. He was insulted. Josh was his direct rival. Laura shouldn't be dueling tongues with *him.*

Suddenly he scented Ms. Argent and glanced in the mirror above the row of sinks. She was standing at the entrance of the boys' locker room. He hitched a breath, reacting to how hot she looked. A beach towel was wrapped around her body like a dress, showing off her sculpted legs.

He was still dripping wet in his Speedo and he turned slightly. He held up a finger—*one minute*—and was very grateful that Ms. Argent didn't have superior hearing, like werewolves. Otherwise she would hear Laura sputtering and threatening to rip off various parts of his body when the assembled pack went on the big hunt.

"This is so you can do something slutty," Laura said.

"Sort of," Derek said noncommittally.

"With a *human*."

"So what? You have."

"I have not. Not . . . that."

He lowered his voice. "I'm not doing . . . *that*." Although he really, really wanted to. "We're just going to talk." Laura snorted. "We *are*," he insisted.

She huffed. "Okay. Okay, even though it's inconvenient. I have a lot of studying to do and I'll tell Mom I need to go to the library. She won't care. But you have to promise me that you'll delete that picture and I *will* be checking your phone."

"Okay," he said. She'd probably kill him when she found out he'd been lying to her, but it would be worth it.

He hung up and pretended not to see Ms. Argent in the mirror. Then he counted to five before he turned around to give her the good news. He knew he couldn't act all over-eager. She wouldn't respect that. But he was so happy that it was difficult not to.

When he did face her, he worked very hard at not grinning ear to ear.

"All set. Let's go," he said.

He left the huge grin for her.

Oh, sweetie, getting your attention is like shooting fish in a barrel, Kate thought as she drove Derek in her car to her apartment. It was across the street from a bar, which, from her point of view, was convenient for when she wanted to hang out with the grown-ups. She was wearing a pair of jeans, heeled boots, and a black low-cut cashmere sweater. *I can practically hear you slobbering. It's like you're a big puppy dog and I am a juicy steak.*

She had taken off her pendant just in case he might know what it was and it was resting safely inside her purse. It showed the Beast of Gévaudan, the murderer that had begun the feud between the hunters and the werewolves. An Argent family heirloom, it served as a token to remind the hunters that they had taken that pelt, and would take many others through the generations.

The thrill of this new hunt raced through her. The euphoria of the chase. She never, ever got tired of dangling herself in front of males of all kinds. It was no accident that in ancient Greece, the deity in charge of the hunt was a goddess—Artemis.

Beside her, Derek "Aquaman" Hale had his head resting on the back of the seat and his eyes closed. He was really good-looking. This was not going to be the most difficult thing she'd ever done in her life.

He opened his eyes and looked at her as if he couldn't believe his good fortune, and, yeah, he was pretty damn lucky if she did say so. Many had called. Few were chosen.

She parked in the spot allotted to her apartment unit. After she killed the engine, she led him inside. A street-level unit, it was pretty sparsely furnished. She wasn't planning to stay in Beacon Hills all that long.

Just long enough.

"Do you really want coffee?" she asked, as she put down her purse and took off her jacket. "Or would you rather have a beer? I also have wine. I like red wine," she said.

He smiled faintly. "We drink wine on—" He stopped himself. "Special occasions."

"Wine it is." She grinned happily. "I like to have a little something to unwind after I'm at the pool, you know? Lucky thing I live across the street from a bar." She said that to goose him a little, remind him she was a woman, with a woman's needs.

He looked a little worried about having wine, but there was no way she was giving him coffee or even a soda with caffeine in it. He was completely amped already. Any more and he'd probably fly to the moon.

The full moon?

She had her orders, but she had to be sure. Kill werewolves, and you were a hero. Kill people, and you were a mass murderer. The group she was involved with had detected werewolf activity in Beacon Hills, and she just had a feeling about the Hales. Of course, there were several other large families in the area that might make up the pack she was seeking. Derek's furtiveness and hesitation might have nothing to do with her assignment. There were reasons other than being a werewolf for not wanting to bring home someone who was way too old for you.

It hadn't dawned on him to question the motives of a pretty woman who was coming on to him. He believed what he chose to believe. Men—werewolves and humans—were so simple. They always assumed you wanted them. Some fat man on a couch burping and watching cage matches?

Oh, yeah, you wanted him.

A guy who threw you around the room and accused you of cheating on him?

Oh, yeah, you wanted him.

Like a hole through your heart.

But the good one? The one that you really did want?

A flash of rage roared through Kate, but she kept it at bay. She could feel it trying to take over, like a wolf scratching at her door. Rage was not her enemy. Rage got the job done.

In ancient Greece—land of Lycoan, said to be the first werewolf—men who pissed off the goddess Artemis were ripped to shreds by her hunting dogs. Several times a day, Kate dreamed about ripping various people to shreds. Of course, she never acted on it. She left that for others much less able to control their savagery.

Through the entrance to the kitchen, she watched as Sweetie Derek politely moved a packing carton off her sofa and sat down. What a body. Still boyish, but with the sweet promise of a truly splendid man. If she was right about the Hales, Derek would never become a man. Just as he wasn't really a boy. He was a monster hidden inside a human disguise.

If she was right.

She poured two glasses of wine and started to pull open the drawer with the secret ingredient . . . except that he got back off the couch and came into the kitchen, stopping in the doorway as if asking permission to enter.

"Well, hello," Kate said. She shut the drawer and handed him one of the glasses. Ruby red, just like blood. Funny thing about werewolves. When you shot them or cut them open, their blood was red, just like humans'.

"What shall we toast to?" she asked him, smiling as he

stared shyly at the wine in his glass, as if drinking together signaled another step in their dance. A closer step. Which it did. That was why people drank together.

When he shrugged his shoulders, she leaned against the counter, giving him a nice view, and said, "How about to life, love, and the pursuit?"

She waited for his response. He was staring at her body. Wanting her. Intimidated by her.

She loved it.

"The pursuit of happiness?" he said, as if he assumed she'd forgotten the actual expression.

"Sure. That's worth pursuing," she said.

They clinked glasses. And drank the wine. Derek was used to it; they had specific rituals for each new moon, including drinking wine and eating traditional delicacies. Wolf Moon was the most special. It was a time for family reunions and reestablishing pack unity. It was also the night for issuing challenges and reordering the hierarchy of the pack.

The night he would kick Josh's ass.

He wanted to tell Ms. Argent all about it. She probably liked athletic men. In human form, he and Josh would run through a set of contests based on strength, speed, and endurance. When the moon rose, they would battle in werewolf form for dominance. The whole pack would watch, and howl in support and approval as the two displayed their cunning and prowess. Challenges kept the pack strong. Werewolves had to be able to take down prey, and defend themselves on the hunt. And, should hunters ever come to their door, they had to be able to defend themselves from the humans.

If anyone ever attacked her, I'd rip out his throat, he thought. She probably had no idea just how wild the world could be. He wanted to shield her, protect her. The pack looked out for its own. The loyalty to the pack went far deeper than what most humans felt for their blood relatives. His Uncle Peter said that the humans were fickle and weak. When they were threatened, they panicked and scattered. Werewolves worked together to take out powerful enemies.

Like hunters. They'd been clashing with hunters for centuries.

"Want another glass of wine, Derek?" she asked him.

He checked the time on his cell phone. He had at least two hours to go.

"I'm having seconds," she said.

"Oh, then yes, please," he said. He drank it down so she wouldn't have to wait and handed the glass to her. She put her knee on the couch as she took it, smiling down at him. He was aware of her scent and the welcoming warmth of her body heat.

"Would you like something to eat?" she asked. "Sandwich? I have roast beef."

He was really hungry. He nodded.

"Thanks," he said.

He watched as she walked back into the kitchen, her hips swaying, and he smiled faintly to himself. Sure, he was nervous, but this was really *cool.* He thought about taking a picture of himself on her couch with his phone but he felt like it might put her in danger. It was awesome that she was willing to take a chance just to be with him. She could get fired, even jailed if things . . . if they happened.

He rose, fidgety and excited, not sure what to do or say when she came back. Was she waiting for him to make the next move?

He wandered around the room. It wasn't very big, and it was filled with cartons. Trying to be casual, he glanced down a short, narrow hall to where her bedroom must be. Just thinking about it made his blood race, and he wiped his face with his hand. He was feeling sweaty and too hot. He caught himself walking a couple of steps down the hall and turned around. Coffee, she had said. Getting to know each other.

And he wanted that. He really did. But he was a young werewolf in his prime, and it was becoming difficult for him to keep himself under control. He checked his fingernails. Had they lengthened? He rubbed his tongue along the edges of his canine teeth. Sharper?

"Here we go," she said, and he darted back into the room as if she'd caught him doing something wrong. She was walking back from the kitchen with a tray. On it were two sandwiches and their wineglasses. The smell of the meat made his stomach growl, and he coughed to hide the sound.

Then she set it all down on her coffee table. She picked up half of her sandwich and he did the same. He took a bite, tasting the rare flesh, mayonnaise, and mustard. He tried to have good manners, chewing with his mouth closed, but he was ravenous.

He swallowed it. She raised her brows. "Good?" she asked.

Nodding, he took another bite, then chased it with his

wine. A couple more bites, and the half-sandwich was gone. As he set down his wineglass, he saw that she'd only taken a couple of dainty nibbles, and he felt like a pig, rushing through his meal.

He eyed the second half hungrily, but made no move to take it. She smiled and took another bite, then sipped her wine.

Silence fell between them. He was hungry, agitated, and his body was humming with excitement. The thought of the juicy meat in her mouth excited him. Wouldn't it be cool if they became a couple and he brought her home to meet the pack? Even better, what if she joined the pack? His Alpha—his father—could give her the Bite. Of course she would live through it. He pictured them running together beneath the full moon. He could imagine her fierce, proud howl as she sought her mate. *Him.* That would be *amazing.*

Josh would be incredibly jealous. Having a mate would bring Derek status.

Maybe she could get the Bite on Wolf Moon, he thought. That would be so awesome. She probably wouldn't be ready that soon, but wouldn't it be great?

She seemed to be taking forever to eat the first half of her sandwich, savoring every morsel. He felt kind of stupid sitting there, waiting for her to finish. He didn't know what to do with his hands. How to sit. She'd invited him there. She'd wanted to get to know him better. But they weren't even talking to each other.

Then she was done, and he eagerly picked up the other half of his sandwich. He felt obvious and silly but he'd committed to waiting, and the wait was over. He sank his teeth into the meat. Thinking about Ms. Argent as a werewolf had excited him. He knew he had to be careful. Knew he couldn't make the shift in front of her. At least, not yet.

He would have to have his Alpha's permission, and he would probably have to bring her to their underground chamber beneath their house, where she could watch him in contained safety. That was where the Hale werewolves went when it wasn't okay to run in the woods. When there were too many humans, or when the young werewolves, like him, seemed especially volatile. He was sixteen, and he was finishing human puberty. When hormones were racing through him, turning him into a man, it was hard for him to stay in control.

Sometimes the Alpha separated the young werewolf males from the rest of the pack if he thought that in their frenzy they might forget how young and untested they really were, and foolishly challenge him for dominance. That was a generous act on his dad's part. He had heard of some packs where the Alpha deliberately tried to stir up the teenagers so he could get rid of them through a challenge—but those were dysfunctional packs.

"I want to know all about you," Ms. Argent said, breaking his reverie as he took another bite of sandwich. He realized that the entire time he had been devouring flesh, he had been staring at her. "Your favorite color, your lucky number, when your birthday is." She daintily pressed a napkin against her lips. "Guess what my favorite color is."

Why did she have to ask him a question when his mouth was full? He chewed quickly, swallowed, and said, "Um, pink?"

"Green." She smiled and surveyed his face as if it were her marked territory. "Like your eyes. But there's brown in them, too. At first I thought they might be blue. They're very expressive."

Whoa. She liked his eyes. And she had spent a lot of time studying him. Tingles played at the small of his back and along his cheeks, and she smiled as if she knew how much her words had affected him.

Then she fluttered her lashes and said, "Now tell me. What is *your* favorite color?"

She held her head still, as if inviting him to look. Inviting him in. For a dizzying moment it seemed as if there was nothing in the world but her lovely, lovely eyes. That they were like moons for him to race beneath, proud, wild, free.

"Your eyes are green, too," he said.

"Good answer." She tore off a piece of her sandwich and popped it into his mouth like a piece of candy. Then she ate a little nibble, too, clearly enjoying the taste.

"Do you believe in fate? That some things are just meant to happen?" she asked him.

"I—I don't know," he answered. He wanted to tell her that he was pretty sure he believed in love at first sight. But maybe she would laugh and tell him that what he wasn't feeling was love, but a stupid little teenage crush that meant nothing.

No, he thought. *Ms. Argent would never say something so cruel. And besides, maybe . . . maybe she believes in love at first sight, too.*

"So, have you been swimming long?" she asked him.

He was grateful that she'd asked him another question.

He needed something, anything to distract him from his thoughts. He was a little afraid he might blurt something out that would reveal how he felt, and it would turn out to be the wrong thing. He didn't want to mess this up. But suddenly he was overcome with the idea that he *would* mess it up. He was so nervous even contemplating that that part of him wanted to run away now, before he could wreck it. But of course everything else urged him to stay, and never, ever leave.

"Derek?" She peered at him. "Swimming?"

"Most of my life," he managed to answer.

She ran her gaze up and down his body. He squeezed the edge of his plate hard. He pulled in his stomach and pushed back his shoulders as discreetly as he could. He wanted to look good for her.

"It shows," she said. And for a moment he couldn't remember what she had asked him about. Swimming. Lap after lap, to burn off the excess energy. To be able to maintain in the human world. To stay disconnected from the ordinary humans who weren't in his family.

"You've got a great swimmer's body and you really know your . . . strokes." She rested her head on her arm, gazing at him. "You seem driven when you swim."

"There's just so much pressure," he blurted, and then he stopped, afraid he had just said the wrong thing. He could never talk about his double life with anyone outside the pack. And if he complained about typical kid stuff, she might think he wasn't mature enough to handle an adult relationship.

"The pressure can be enormous," she agreed. She leaned

forward, placing her forearms on her thighs. He was aware of how her sweater front bunched, and he could see her cleavage. He made himself let go of his plate so that he wouldn't break it and clenched his left hand tightly against his own thigh.

"I hated high school," she said. "They tell you you're responsible for your life and then you come home and find out your family's moving. Or that your parents are getting divorced. And you have no say in any of it."

"I know," he said, nodding. She got it—at least the human side of it.

"It's such a mishmash, and you have to deal with all of it," she went on. "And the people you have to hang out with, day after day. Some kids in high school are babies and others are all grown up, ready for the real world. Like you."

Wow, could she really tell that? She was probably just flattering him.

But you're in her apartment, he reminded himself. *She must like something about you. She's risking her job just to be with you.*

With you.

She leaned toward him and took a sip out of his wineglass. As she looked over the rim at him, he thought he would drown in her beautiful green eyes.

"So let me ask you, Derek," she said. "*Are* you ready?

He set down his sandwich. His heart was about to burst out of his chest. His body was quivering and trembling. He felt as if he were burning up.

"Yes," he whispered. "I'm ready."

CHAPTER FOURTEEN

In Jackson's living room, Lydia sat tied to a Louis XIV gilt wooden chair while the two robbers—Ski Mask and Gravelly Voice—methodically went through each room of the Whittemores' home. They knew their valuables, skipping the big plasma TV for the elegant, if plain, sterling silver tea set. They bypassed the matted prints Mr. Whittemore had given Mrs. Whittemore before they could afford fine art and took the original oils and acrylics. Sooner or later, they would take the chair she was sitting on. It was a valuable antique.

Lydia had found out there was a third thief, one she had nicknamed Worker Bee, because his entire job consisted of loading the Whittemores' belongings into whatever enormous vehicle they had brought with them. She hadn't seen him at all, and she hadn't seen the faces of Ski Mask and Gravelly Voice. She was praying that meant that she would come out of this alive.

She had no idea how much time had passed. It seemed like a lifetime ago since they had hit her and threatened her with a gun. They'd asked her over and over and over again if she was alone in the house. And despite the fact that there were two cars in the driveway, they believed her. Either they hadn't seen Danny's Lexus behind her car or they had discounted it for some reason. She told them that she was Jackson's girlfriend—true—and that she didn't know where he was, so she had come to his house to look for him—also true.

At first she kept expecting to hear police sirens. Surely Damon or Danny would call 911. Then it dawned on her that the boys must be able to see or hear inside, because Ski Mask had told her that that they had accomplices planted in cars along the route to the sheriff's station, and they would get plenty of warning before the cops arrived—enough time to blow her away. So Danny and Damon must have been afraid to call for help.

Call anyway. Just explain, she thought, trying to transmit her thoughts to them via ESP or something. But in reality, she doubted she would call the police, either. Look how long it had taken to find one maniac mountain lion that had been killing people all over Beacon Hills. And the sheriff hadn't killed it. Allison's father had.

She still remembered the day Jackson had shown her every piece of the house's state-of-the-art security system. These guys seemed to know about it, too. So she doubted there was some superhero or private security guard just waiting for the right moment to crash through the skylight above Lydia's head and save her.

She swallowed hard and glanced up at said skylight . . .

. . . and, framed by moonlight, Danny and Damon stared back down at her.

She nearly fell over backward in the chair, but somehow

the thieves didn't notice her shock. Ski Mask was busily going through the kitchen drawers while Gravelly Voice carried an enameled Chinese vase to the garage loading area. She composed herself, then peered upward, having no clue whatsoever about what they were trying to tell her. They kept gesturing and opening their mouths very wide as if they wanted to communicate something to her. Were they going to go for help? That would mean leaving her here alone. Tied up. With criminals who had threatened to kill her. What if one of their accomplices saw the boys on the roof?

Then both boys disappeared. She braced herself—for what, she didn't know—and realized the situation was changing. Forcing her emotions at bay, her logical mathematician's mind formed a decision tree of actions, reactions, and outcomes. She tried to think about what she knew about Danny and Damon. Danny was Jackson's best friend, which meant that he wasn't a loser. He was smart, and strong. He was the lacrosse team's goalie, which meant he was willing to deliberately stand in the path of a hard rubber ball going a hundred miles an hour. She knew the scary stats: in the last twenty-five years, almost two dozen lacrosse players had died of cardiac arrest from taking balls to the chest. There were few people in the world tougher than lacrosse goalies—and Danny was the toughest. Danny put the *M* in *macho*, that was for sure.

So in a situation like this, what would a guy like that do?

He's going to take them on.

She didn't know if she should cheer or scream. It was one thing to take a ball to the chest, quite another to take a bullet.

But she was absolutely positive that was what they were trying to tell her. What did they want her to do? Sit tight?

I don't think so.

It was one thing to sit quietly and observantly because it had seemed like her best option, but it was quite another thing to be a sitting duck. If the guys launched an offensive, the first thing she would do to stop them if she were a thief was put a gun to the head of the pretty strawberry blonde.

So I have to make sure that doesn't happen, she decided.

So, decision tree: if she wanted to get herself free, what should she do?

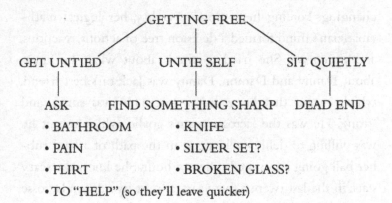

GETTING FREE

GET UNTIED   UNTIE SELF   SIT QUIETLY

ASK   FIND SOMETHING SHARP   DEAD END

- BATHROOM
- PAIN
- FLIRT
- TO "HELP" (so they'll leave quicker)

- KNIFE
- SILVER SET?
- BROKEN GLASS?

Lydia glanced back up at the skylight, wishing she could have understood what Damon and Danny were trying to tell her.

"We should get cracking," Gravelly Voice said as he returned from the garage.

Ski Mask came out of the kitchen with the large silver platter with the rosettes that Jackson's mother had served the Thanksgiving turkey on. The two men stood facing each other. They lowered their voices to near-whispers. Gravelly Voice looked over his shoulder at her, then muttered something to Ski Mask.

They're trying to decide what to do with me, Lydia realized. Her fear level shot sky-high. It was time to solve her problem. What kind of men were they? What was her best option at getting them to untie her without hurting her?

She did the math:

Question: What kind of men did these guys think they were?

Factors:

1. They planned the robbery in advance.
2. They had the security alarm codes.
3. They lured Jackson away with some scam about his birth parents. But Jackson was smart and suspicious. They'd have had to plead their case pretty well.
4. They knew what to steal and what to leave.

Conclusion: They were thorough.

Factors:

5. They had been surprised to see her, but had taken swift action.
6. They had been careful to keep their faces concealed so they wouldn't have to kill her.

But now they were muttering about her.

Conclusion one: They were having second thoughts about leaving her alive, but they were discussing it calmly.

Conclusion two: They were smart and ruthless. But they

also didn't act rashly. So flirting, asking to go to the bathroom, or offering to help probably wouldn't work.

So Lydia took action. Summoning her best acting skills—and Lydia had put on some stellar performances in her day, acting like an airhead for Jackson's sake—she smiled to herself. She made it a secretive, sly smile, holding it just long enough so that when Gravelly Voice looked at her, he saw it. Then she made a show of letting it slip.

She was absolutely terrified, but she pretended not to realize that Gravelly Voice had seen her smile.

"Hey," he said, stomping over to her, "what's the big joke?"

"Oh." She made her eyes big and round, and swallowed hard. "Um. Nothing." She fluttered her lashes, hoping that wasn't laying it on too thick.

He gestured to Ski Mask, who came over.

"She was smiling," Gravelly Voice reported.

They both stared down at her through their ski masks, and she made herself keep her head. She would not panic. She would play this out.

"Why?" Ski Mask demanded. He pointed his gun at her. "Tell me."

She focused on data collection. Ski Mask was the boss. Ski Mask was the one who was armed. She couldn't believe it had taken her this long to realize that Gravelly Voice didn't have a gun.

Ski Mask bent over and put the gun against her head, like before, and it terrified her just as badly as before. All he had to do was pull the trigger. If Damon and Danny chose this moment to attack, she would be dead.

"You can't blame me for forgetting," she said in a high, little-girl voice. Her heart was pounding so hard she was afraid she would faint. She had to keep it together, play this through. She remembered days driving the golf cart at the country club for her father while he selected the proper club and took his time lining up his shot.

"Always play it through," her father said.

"What did you forget?" Ski Mask asked, looming over her. "Tell me now, or I'll kill you."

But he wouldn't. She knew it. Because while he was ruthless, he was not impulsive. They hadn't killed her when they'd first invaded the house, and they had a reason to keep her alive right now: they had to know the secret she was convincing them she had.

"Promise not to hurt me if I tell you," she said.

"No," the guy said, pushing the gun against her forehead.

She shut her eyes against a disabling stab of panic. It was all right to let them know that she was afraid, but not okay to lose control. She had to stay in control.

"Okay. Well, Jackson thought it would be funny to spy on his parents. So he installed a Web cam."

The guy slapped her with his free hand and she gasped, shocked. She burst into real tears.

"Where is it?"

"I don't know," she replied. "I know he watches them on his computer."

"So it's not running right now," Gravelly Voice said, but he sounded uncertain. "Right?"

"I *told* you to tell me everything," Ski Mask said. He threw back his hand to slap her again, then seemed to think the better of it and lowered his arm to his side. "You kept this from us. *Lied* to us." He was indignant.

"I forgot about it. Really," she said, as tears tumbled down her cheeks. "I swear I did."

"We need to check it out," Ski Mask said. "Go into his room and turn on his computer. See if you can see it."

Gravelly Voice didn't move.

Ski Mask stared at him. *"Well?"*

"Um," Gravelly Voice said, "I'm not sure how."

"You're useless," Ski Mask barked at him. But he made no move to go into Jackson's room, either.

"Do *you* know how to see it on his computer?" Ski Mask asked her.

This was the moment when she had to put on the best performance of her life. She lowered her head and moved her shoulders.

"I . . . guess," she said reluctantly. As if not every single part of her was screaming at him to untie her. "If you go into his room, I could call out to you how to look at it."

"Okay—" Gravelly Voice said, but Ski Mask cut him off.

"No yelling," he said.

But they had yelled earlier. He had shouted at her that he was going to kill her if she moved a muscle. So maybe things were changing for them, too. They were getting cautious. It was possible—no, *probable*—they had timed the robbery, and they had been there too long. So maybe they were starting to get desperate.

"I'm going to untie you," Ski Mask said. She kept her face blank. "This is real life. This is not the movies. You don't know kung fu and I've got a gun. I don't know how much you know about guns, but this one has a silencer on it. No one will hear it go off. The next sound will be the cracking of your skull just before it enters your brain. Got it?"

Lydia bit her lip. She was almost afraid to be untied, to walk with this man holding a weapon. She tried not to stare at the gun as Gravelly Voice went behind the chair and untied her hands, but she was pretty sure it wasn't equipped with a silencer. It didn't look long enough. But on the other hand, despite all the hundreds of hours she had spent watching cop shows and action movies, she couldn't bring to mind exactly what a silencer looked like.

After Gravelly Voice finished untying her, her hands stung like crazy. That was the blood rushing back into them. She stood, feeling incredibly dizzy, and the room seemed to tilt to the side as Ski Mask stepped away from her and she shuffled away from the chair.

Now what? Now what? she thought, flush with victory but trying to work out the next step in her mind. *We're going to Jackson's room. What's in his room that I could use to defend myself? He has trophies. Could I smash a trophy in this guy's face? Is that just wishful thinking? Could I send a message when I turn on Jackson's computer? Activate his Face Talk?*

She had to think on her feet, literally, as she stood on the threshold of Jackson's room. She saw it almost the way a stranger would, and fresh panic surged through her. She had to make this work. Had to make it count.

Ski Mask turned off the light that she herself had turned on. The three stood in darkness . . . except that Jackson's curtains were open. Maybe she could signal where she was to Danny and Damon.

And then what?

"Don't try *anything*," Ski Mask ordered her. Then he gripped her arm tightly. "No heroics. I'll shoot you. Now walk to his desk, sit down, and turn on his computer."

She thought about pretending to stumble and asking him to turn on a light. But she remembered her logical conclusions: this guy was smart. She didn't want to find herself being harmed because he saw through her charade. So she swayed nervously through Jackson's room, felt for the chair—had a wild, insane moment were she fantasized about grabbing it and whirling in a half circle, knocking both of them over like bowling pins—and then pulled out the chair and sat down. Her hands found the keyboard, and she knew the on button was the upper right key.

Still in the dark, just before she turned it on, she pulled the monitor sideways as quickly and as discreetly as she could, angling it toward the window, and prayed that the light would reveal what was going on inside. Or at the very least, serve as a signal to Danny and Damon about where she was.

"Don't do anything stupid," Ski Mask said, and she was afraid he'd caught her moving the monitor. "Turn it on *now*."

Lydia pressed the power button.

Be watching, she mentally ordered Danny and Damon.

Jackson was slowly coming awake. His head was pounding, and he felt sick to his stomach. He heard someone crying, and he figured that was not a good thing. Then he realized his gag was off, but the handcuffs were still on, and his aching head was in someone's lap. He half turned, grunting against the pain.

A hand went over his mouth. He looked up to see Cassie staring down at him, her face streaked with tears. She gave her head a shake and pressed the forefinger of her free hand across her lips. Her blond hair was making a curtain around her face, so it was all he could see.

"He didn't see your face, Bailey," she said. "And even if he did, what's he going to say? He doesn't know who you are."

"You're right. He didn't see me. But he saw *you*. You idiot." It was Hunter Gramm—or rather, Bailey somebody.

"So what?" Cassie said. "I don't have a record."

"Don't be an idiot. I *do*. And you're my girlfriend."

"Even if they get a description out to the police, we'll be long gone. We can just dump him somewhere while he's unconscious."

"Mack should have left that damn Porsche behind. It's too noticeable. I'm going to kick his ass for that," Bailey said. "But . . . Jackson Whittemore is a danger to us, baby. You know we can't just let him go."

"Yes, yes, we can," she begged.

"Maybe we can make it look like a carjacking," Bailey said.

Jackson's eyes bulged. *He's planning my murder. I have to get out of here* now. He started to raise his head, and Cassie pushed it back down.

A cell phone rang, then was cut off. Losing his cool, Jackson tried to jerk upright. She pushed harder on his head.

"Yeah." Bailey paused, listening. "Are you freaking kidding me?" he said. "And you let her get on his computer?" He swore.

Jackson listened hard. Someone—a her—was on "his" computer. Whose? What was going on? Bailey was obviously working with someone. Doing . . .

He shut his eyes tightly. His parents were away. He was here. Which left the possibility that Lydia was at his house, on his computer, with the caller.

I told her I was coming back soon. She probably went to my house to wait for me.

His heart felt as if it had just flopped over inside his rib cage. He yanked on his handcuffs, trying to pull them apart, and Cassie clapped both her hands over his nose and mouth and stared at hard at him. He looked up at her, and she licked her lips, listening.

"Spy camera? That's . . ." Bailey trailed off. "Are you watching her? She's not sending a message? Shut it down. *Now.*"

Unable to breathe, Jackson struggled quietly against her hands, and she slid them down off his nose. She moved her mouth, but it was too dark for him to make out what she was saying. Then they glided under a streetlight.

I. Will. Help. You.

He nodded to let her know he understood. He wanted to know what was going on at his house. Had to know. He was so afraid for Lydia.

Then Bailey shouted into the phone, "What's happening?"

CHAPTER FIFTEEN

Beacon Hills
Six Years Ago

I'm ready," Derek said, as he finished his second glass of wine.

Then Ms. Argent put one hand on either side of his face, smiled into his eyes, and kissed him. Her lips were so soft, and so warm, and it felt so good. So amazingly good.

He had to be careful. But he was losing himself in the kiss and images flashed through his head, animalistic and fierce; he wanted to do all kinds of things to her and he didn't dare. He was going to lose control. He was going to hurt her. But he couldn't stop kissing her.

She trailed her mouth across the hollow of his cheek to his ear and whispered, "I love this. I love how dangerous it is. It excites me."

And then she pulled away. "Oh, Derek," she murmured, and she looked into his eyes, as if searching for something. "I just . . . I know we said we'd take it slow. That we'd have coffee," she murmured. "And instead we had the wine, and it's loosened my inhibitions, and you're just so incredible."

She licked her lips and smoothed back her hair. "Okay. I'll behave." She pursed her lips. "So, ah, what else do you like to do besides swim?"

Kiss you, Derek thought. Then something felt wrong. His stomach cramped. The back of his throat started burning. And his eyes stung. He tried to ignore it. He wanted to kiss her some more.

His stomach contracted. His throat filled with acid. He was going to throw up.

Oh, God, I can't barf in front of her, he thought.

He got to his feet. She moved away, her brows knitting. "I've offended you," she said. "I'm sorry, Derek."

"No. I'm just not feeling well," he told her. "May I use your bathroom?"

"Sure. It's down the hall. Do you need something? A glass of water?"

He started to say yes, but he didn't know what was happening. He was lurching down the hall, his stomach churning. He was so embarrassed that he wanted to die. He felt so sick that he wanted to die.

He lifted the lid on the toilet, fell to his knees, and threw up. He fumbled for the sink faucet and turned it on full blast so she wouldn't hear him. He flushed the toilet, too, and then he vomited some more.

It couldn't have been the meat. Werewolves could smell bad carrion and knew to stay away from it. Maybe the mayo was bad. Or maybe it was just nerves.

He felt so unbelievably stupid. He threw up some more,

wincing from the pain and grimacing because he was barfing so incredibly loudly. She had to be hearing it. Way to ruin their whole evening.

I was just about to have sex for the first time in my life. I know it.

And instead he was in Ms. Argent's bathroom, puking his guts out. How was he ever going to face her again? Wiping sweat from his forehead, he lifted his head and studied the tiny rectangular bathroom above her shower stall. Too small. Maybe there was a back door and he could just sneak out and never see her again. No more pool.

There was a rap on the door. He shut his eyes tight and hoped it was locked. If she came in there and saw him, smelled *it* . . .

He didn't say anything. There was another knock.

"Derek? Would you like a glass of water?"

He was taken aback. She was being cool about it. Not asking him if he was okay—because he obviously wasn't— and not treating him like a kid.

"Yeah," he rasped. He laid his forehead on the seat and let out a sigh. The worst seemed to be over. He healed quickly. Whatever had been in his system would be dealt with in short order.

Unless it's something poisonous to werewolves, he thought. But like what? He hadn't smelled anything like wolfsbane.

"Just a minute," he said.

He rose from the toilet, flushed it again, then went to her shower stall and opened the window above it. The crisp night are refreshed him a little. He turned the water at the sink and scooped some into his mouth, then swooshed it around and spit it out. Then he opened the door and held out his hand for the water glass without looking at her.

He drank it down, poured himself another, and drank that, too. He didn't want to mess up her towels, so he cleaned around his mouth with toilet paper. Then he dampened some more sheets and wiped his face.

She was waiting for him in the living room with a concerned expression. He wished the floor would open him up and swallow him.

"There's a virus going around at school," she said. She was holding some car keys. "Do you want to meet your sister? I can drive you anywhere you want to go."

Mortified, Derek shook his head. She was booting him. No surprise there. He was totally disgusting.

"I'll call her on my cell," he said. He put a hand on the knob of the front door. "I'm . . . I'm sorry," he blurted out, speaking so softly he wasn't sure she would hear him.

"Oh, please, don't, Derek," she said. "These things happen. Maybe it was the roast beef."

"No," he said. "It wasn't."

She cocked her head. "How do you know?"

Smooth, he told himself. "Well, you're not sick," he said.

She grinned at him and put her hand over her flat stomach. She had really nice boobs. He was ashamed of himself for noticing them at a time like this. He'd thought he'd get a chance to see them, touch them. He had totally blown it.

"Ah, but I have a cast-iron stomach," she said. "It takes a lot to make me feel sick."

"Well, I'm glad you didn't, um, that nothing happened to you."

She cocked her head. "You really are the sweetest, you know? I had no idea you were so thoughtful. Few men are."

There it was, her calling him a man again. Was she just trying to let him down easy? Would he really ever see her again, except at school?

"Let me drive you somewhere," she said.

He felt as if she was treating him like a kid. He had a license. He just didn't have a car. He wanted to make sure she knew that, but he knew it would sound stupid. Just about anything he told her would sound like he was trying to prove himself. Besides, he didn't want her to come near him, smell him. He was gross.

"I'm going to get some air, and then I'll call my sister," he said, trying to sound decisive.

She jingled the keys. "Well, if you're sure."

"Yeah. I am." He opened the door. "Thanks for everything." He was so crushed.

"See if there's a car you can borrow," she said. "A friend's, maybe? We'll try it again. Maybe tomorrow?"

Whoa. He almost shouted for joy. He couldn't believe how cool she was being. She was going to give him another chance.

"Um, after swimming?" he asked. She had to be at the pool. It was her job.

"Yes. But don't overdo it," she said. "You might be coming down with something."

"Okay, thank you," he said in a rush. He turned away as he opened the door, in case there was something on his face or clothes. But he was so happy he wanted to throw his arms around her and cover her with kisses.

"Good night," she said sweetly. With his back to her, he felt her fingers trailing through his hair. "Let me know that you get home safe."

That sounded like an adult talking to a kid. Then he reminded himself that his parents checked in with each other like that. It was a normal thing to do when you cared about somebody.

She cares about me. After I threw up in her house, she still wants to be with me. He couldn't believe how lucky he was. And how understanding she was being.

"I don't know your phone number," he said.

"I'll call yours and then we'll have each other's," she said.

He gave her his number. She punched it in and his phone rang. He didn't have a jazzy little ringtone like some people had. It was just one of the boring generic sounds that came with the phone. He wondered what her ringtone sounded like.

"Got you," she said. "Think I'll keep you."

Derek went hot all over. He tried to act flirtatious like her and smile back, maybe reach out and do . . . what? He had no idea how to act like that. He hardly ever even spoke at school. She didn't know that about him. All she knew was that he swam and he had an older sister named Laura. Maybe now she was beginning to realize that that was all he had going for him.

He wished with all his heart that he hadn't thrown up. He didn't want to leave. What if she changed her mind between now and tomorrow? Was she just being polite and pretending to still be interested in him? Maybe she thought he was a douche kid who couldn't hold his liquor. He wanted to tell her that he was part of an incredible, amazing world filled with beings she wouldn't be able to believe were real. That when he transformed into werewolf mode, he could run ten times faster than he could swim, and that his endurance was amazing. Shifted, he was so strong he could lift her with one hand and carry her in his arms for miles.

He wanted to tell her that the howl of a werewolf was better than any ringtone, any song, on earth. Standing beneath the full moon with others of his kind—his pack, his moonborn family—he felt such an incredible sense of belonging that there weren't even words for it in human language.

She knew how to connect with humans on a level that baffled him, but if only they were both werewolves, he would know exactly what to do and say to offer his loyalty and form a bond with her. Like wolves, werewolves mated for life. He imagined running through the forest with her, the magical light of the full moon glowing down on her pelt. Did she want him to be her boyfriend? The behavioral cues of humans were ambiguous and difficult to comprehend. But the instinctual gestures of werewolves were direct, honest, and definite. If they were werewolves, he would be able to display his dominance and attractiveness, preen for her and impress her.

Maybe someday, he thought. That would be the happiest day of his life.

"Penny for your thoughts," she said.

He swallowed down everything he was thinking and feeling as reality came crashing down on him. She was human, and he needed to relate to her on a human level.

"I-I'm . . ." He didn't know what to say. *I'm sorry I was so repulsive? Are you just being nice to me to salvage my ego? Do you really want me to come over tomorrow?*

He was afraid to ask her anything. Afraid she would simply laugh at him.

"I'll see you," he said, lifting his chin a little, trying to look unfazed.

"Can't wait," she replied. She bent forward as if to kiss him but he jerked, and she shifted away from him.

I smell, he thought.

The door clicking behind him sounded so final. *Please, please give me a second chance.*

Putting his hands into his pockets, he began to walk down the street. He looked in the direction of her apartment. A light came on in a window but he wasn't sure it was part of her unit. Werewolves had good spatial skills—they were able to assess the shape and size of rooms, dens, and enclosures, notice entrances and exits. But when he tried to remember the layout of Kate's apartment, all he could think about was the hall and the bathroom—the longest walk of his life.

Without being fully aware of what he was doing, Derek broke into a jog. He hadn't swum long enough to burn off all the adrenaline from the day, and now he was loaded with tension, both physical and emotional. The evening breezes around him seemed to spark his nerve endings, and he sizzled and burned until he felt like he was on fire.

Ms. Argent, he thought. He couldn't let himself think her first name. It was forbidden territory, even though . . . even though . . .

Maybe I misunderstood. Maybe we weren't going to have sex.

He kept running, easing his anxiety, feeling cut off in the human world from his pack. His cell phone was in his pocket and he gripped it tightly, preparing to call his sister. But he'd never tell her why he was done early, and she'd tease him unmercifully even if she'd didn't know the details, because the date had obviously been an epic fail. Right now, he couldn't bear any more humiliation. His and Laura's relationship was both very similar and very different from those of human siblings. They sparred and jabbed for dominance and position, but a deep loyalty ran between them. In the world of Beacon Hills, they were strangers in a strange land. In Laura's mind, she visited her human friends and crushes, but she lived with the pack. So maybe she wouldn't tease him too much.

He kept running, listening to his breath, feeling the rise in his pulse. He wanted to throw back his head and howl, seeking his kind, expressing the confusing and complex layering of his human emotions. Instead, he ran faster, savoring his strength and endurance. He wasn't even sure where he was going.

Farther and farther away from Ms. Argent.

Beacon Hills Hospital loomed ahead on the other side of the intersection, and he placed himself in the grid of the town. When the light turned green, he trotted across. Glancing to the left, he saw a little boy and a couple walking out of the hospital. He detected the odor of sickness. It was coming from the woman. The man and the boy were walking slowly on purpose, to keep pace with her.

"So what does it mean?" the boy asked. Derek could hear him perfectly. "Does it mean she's all better?"

"Yes," said the man, but Derek detected the quaver of a lie in his voice.

"'Remission' means that there's no evidence of new disease," the woman said.

The boy was quiet for a moment. Then he said, "How's that different from 'all better'?"

The added smell of distress rolled off the woman. Derek knew she was the wife, the mother, and that she was afraid. She didn't want to upset the boy with the truth.

That she was probably dying.

"It's not different," she said finally. She took the little boy's hand. Most boys his age would protest and refuse to hold hands with a parent, but this one clung tightly. All three of them were frightened, but they were drawing a little comfort from each other. Some. But not enough.

A car alarm chirruped as it was disabled. The man went to the passenger side of a Toyota and opened door. He held out his arm to the woman.

"After you, Mrs. Stilinksi," he said.

"Thank you, Deputy Stilinksi," she replied. She gripped his forearm as she cautiously bent her knees and sat on the seat.

The boy thrust open the backseat door and sat behind her. Derek watched as he straightened his fingers as if to touch her hair, then pulled them back and made two fists in his lap. His foot beat out a staccato against the floor, a nervous tic. The boy was a bundle of nerves, just like him.

The man got behind the wheel and the little family drove off. The stench of sickness lingered in the air. Humans got sick easily, died even more easily. The thought of Ms.

Argent dying made him stumble. What if there *had* been something wrong with the meat? What if she decided to eat some more of it?

He hung a U and broke into a run, not waiting for the light to change. Cars honked and beeped as they swerved around him. He ignored them, reminding himself not to run too fast or draw attention to himself. But his need to make sure that she was all right as strong as his need to breathe.

He got to her door and raised his hand to knock. Then he heard her talking.

"I confirmed it, and I don't think we should wait to hear back from them," she was saying. "You know what happened. We need to make it right."

He didn't know what he was talking about, and he was curious, but he figured it wasn't his business. The urge to protect his own still poured through his veins, and he stood panting on her porch, unsure of what to do. He was just about to leave when he stumbled into a metal trash can that hadn't been there before.

"Hello?" she called, and the door opened. She was standing in a red satin robe. Her feet were bare.

She blinked, startled. "Derek," she said. "Are you all right?"

He was covered in sweat, and she was lovely. He ran his hands through his hair, unable to explain, at a loss for what to say.

"Oh, God," he blurted out, "I'm sorry."

He turned to go, and she put a hand on his shoulder. Molded her fingers around his muscles, and ran her thumb back and forth along the indentation where bone met sinew.

"Hey," she said. "Hey."

He peered up at her, wishing he could just talk to her, tell her everything he was feeling, hoping, fearing. In the parking lot, everything had felt intense and dire; but now, seeing her and knowing she was all right, he didn't know what he had thought he was doing, racing back here.

"I'm—" he said. And he didn't know what he was. He was almost in tears.

He towered over her, even at sixteen, and she gazed up at him took one of his hands with both of hers.

"You're feeling better," she guessed.

He nodded.

She opened the door wider and drew him across the threshold. "You can take a shower," she said. "And I have an extra toothbrush." She laid his hand on her collarbone and trailed her fingers along it. She kept looking at him, as if willing him not to fly apart.

"Okay?" she said.

Wordlessly, he nodded. His moved his hand.

And Ms. Argent shut the night out, and brought him into her den.

CHAPTER SIXTEEN

Beacon Hills
The Present

In Jackson's room, everything happened in a blur.

Something shattered the window as it shot through it fast and hard. The projectile hit Ski Mask hard in the head. As he toppled, his gun went off with a loud bang. Gravelly Voice started yelling and dove to the floor.

Rescue!

Lydia didn't hesitate.

She bolted.

Wordlessly, she charged out of Jackson's room, skidding around a corner as Gravelly Voice bellowed and let fly with a barrage of swearing. Panting, she dashed for the front door just as it burst open. Danny had on his lacrosse padding and Damon was wearing Danny's helmet. There was a ball in the pocket of Danny's lacrosse stick and he shot it hard in the direction she had just come. Lightning fast, he grabbed another one out of the equipment bag.

"Get in my car!" Danny yelled.

Lydia made for Danny's Lexus. The engine was running and the doors were open. They'd planned it out well. Just as she fell into the passenger-side front seat, Danny and Damon flew back out and raced across the courtyard.

Danny turned and shot another ball. Lydia didn't see where it landed. She didn't really look. As Danny leaped into the car, she said, "Call 911."

Danny screeched the car backward. The security gate crept open slowly and as they waited, Danny pulled his phone out of his pocket and handed it to Lydia.

"We heard them talking about accomplices," Damon said. Then Gravelly Voice flew out the front door toward them and Danny floored the car. It just cleared the end of the gate and then Danny put the car in drive as Lydia punched in 911.

The dispatcher answered. On speaker, Lydia told her what had happened, and that the thieves told her they'd planted spies all through Beacon Hills to kill her if she escaped. The dispatcher asked her if there was an alternate route she could take. The woman had the map up and described various streets to Lydia, suggesting that perhaps they could take the road that led to the south.

Toward Beacon Hills Preserve.

"What if there are shooters waiting for us?" Lydia demanded, looking at Danny. He didn't take his eyes off the road. In the back, Damon was sliding from the left side of the car to the right and back again, looking for guys with guns.

"We're sending squad cars," the dispatcher assured her.

"Proceed with caution, but get out of there. I'm staying on the line with you."

Lydia looked at Damon. "Do you have your cell?" He nodded. "Call Jackson."

"Get out of there! Get out!" Bailey shouted into the phone. Then he swore long and hard as he punched in another number.

"Mack, it's falling apart," Bailey bellowed. "Someone shot Del and the girl got away."

Lydia, Jackson thought. He looked up at Cassie, who was ashen. She dug her fingers into his shoulder, then jerked them away as if she'd been branded when he winced. Fresh tears cascaded down her face and she began to sob.

"Bailey, pull over. Let this boy go. Then we can drive away right now and nobody will find us." She sounded as if she knew she was lying. Jackson wondered if Bailey was still wearing his ski mask. He still hadn't see Bailey's face. He opened his mouth to speak, and Cassie pressed her hands over it again.

"I look like a million girls. I barely said two words to him. It'll be okay."

Bailey was silent for a moment. Then he said, "No loose ends."

Jackson stiffened. There was no way he was going down without a fight.

"Help me," he whispered very softly, not sure she could hear him.

"If you kill him, and they catch us, I might never see you again," she said desperately. "Please, *please* let him go. You're *not* a killer."

Bailey didn't answer. Cassie kept crying.

"Stop it!" Bailey shouted at her. "I can't hear myself think."

Then they heard a siren in the distance. Disoriented, his head throbbing, Jackson couldn't tell what direction it was coming from. But the van turned sharply; brakes squealed, and Jackson tried to take advantage and get away from Cassie. But she held him tightly.

"That siren's coming from the north," Bailey said. "It's not for us. No one knows where we are. But we have to turn around and go back the way we came. As soon as we get some distance, we'll have to take care of the situation."

Cassie sobbed for what seemed to Jackson a long time. She put her finger against Jackson's lips. She'd promised to help him, but he was beginning to wonder if she had the backbone to stand up to Bailey. He remembered what she'd said to him in the preserve. She wanted out. Maybe he could help convince her to get out.

"Cassie?" Bailey said sharply.

"Where are we going?" she asked him. "We can't just . . . do it anywhere."

"Maybe we should do it in the van," he replied. "Like right now."

Jackson watched her shaking her head to herself, eyes shutting tightly. She seemed to age years in seconds.

"There are too many cars on the road. Someone will trace the license plate. Maybe we can get back to the preserve," she said. "Meet back up with Mack. Leave this guy there with his Porsche and drive to Mexico, like we planned."

"Maybe it sounds like you're more worried about making sure this guy is okay instead of worrying about us," Bailey said.

"No, baby, of course not," she said quickly.

She fixed Jackson with a serious expression. Then she reached into a pocket in her jacket and pulled out a cell phone, making sure Jackson saw it.

"How's he doing, anyway?" Bailey asked.

"Out cold," she said. "I hope he's not dead already."

"Why? That would solve the problem," Bailey retorted.

"You didn't used to be like this," she said through her tears.

There was a silence. Then he said, "Yeah, I did. You just didn't know it."

"Oh, *God*," she whispered brokenly. "But you said—"

"I said a few things," Bailey cut in. "That didn't mean all of them were true. But I said I loved you, and that *is* the truth."

"Okay," she ground out.

She was clearly in agony. She cried some more, with her entire body. Then she took a deep breath and punched in a number. Jackson couldn't see it, but there were only three numbers: 911? He couldn't hear it ringing. Good thing; then Bailey wouldn't, either.

"Hold on, hanging a sharp left," Bailey said.

The sound of the siren had receded. So no one was coming after them. Or Bailey was outrunning them.

Cassie thumbed in a message on her phone and turned the display window toward Jackson. She had opened her text-messaging bubble and written: *No handcuff key*

He nodded. She typed in more.

Going to push open door. Jump out w u.

His eyes widened. Jump out of a moving vehicle into traffic? He started to shake his head, but he thought about the option: getting shot. He didn't have any recourse, did he?

He pictured himself in traction in a hospital. A doctor telling him to forget lacrosse. To forget *walking*.

Then he imagined himself lying in a coffin with all his friends gathered around, gazing down at him. Lydia sobbing, "At least they were able to conceal the bullet wound."

He thought about the pain of being hit by a car. It was kind of ironic for a guy who played lacrosse to worry about *that*.

Have to move fast, Cassie typed.

Bailey's phone rang, and Cassie jumped a mile. Then she stared down at Jackson and gave him a little nod. She slipped her cell phone into the pocket of his letter jacket.

"Yeah, Mack," Bailey said.

"Now!" Cassie shouted.

Jackson sat upright and pushed himself back against the seat while Cassie dove past him, grabbing at the door handle. She got it to start sliding open when a shot rang out. Jackson looked up to see Bailey aiming his gun at the two of them.

"What the hell?" Bailey shouted.

"No!" she shrieked.

The door slid back, and Cassie put her arm around Jackson's neck, preparing to pull him out with the momentum of her drop as she leaped out of the van. He could see that it wasn't going to work.

There was another shot, and Cassie screamed and slumped. Blood spurted everywhere, coating the inside of the van, and Jackson. Bailey screamed almost as frantically at Cassie and the car began to zigzag wildly down the road. Jackson folded himself over Cassie, trying to make himself less of a target while at the same time shielding her. He had never been so afraid in his life, even when he'd been in the video store and he had found the dead clerk.

"Cassie!" Bailey cried.

The van sped up and bumped and jumped over what felt like acres of stones. Jackson rotated his head and stared through the open door. They had circled back to the preserve, but they were nowhere near the parking lot. He didn't know where they were.

"Get away from her," Bailey yelled at Jackson. He sounded crazed, frantic. "Don't touch her!"

Then the van crashed.

Time stopped as the windshield exploded and metal screeched and folded. A body-slamming jolt smashed Jackson backward, whipping back his already-aching head. Cassie's body cushioned his own as he pitched forward against the back of the front seat, instinctively tucking in his head.

He blacked out for a second, then came to as a shower of glass rained down on him and Cassie. She didn't react.

He smelled gas.

And smoke.

Still handcuffed, Jackson tried to get out, but Cassie was in the way. He strained to lift himself back into the seat for better traction with his feet and saw a roiling billow of thick, gray smoke churning into the open van door. Orange flames licked on the side closest to the back of the van, where the gas tank was, and he began to panic. Cassie lay motionless across his lap. It was very quiet in the front seat. Jackson wondered if Bailey was dead. He so very totally hoped so.

"Cassie, Cassie," he said.

She stirred, moaning. "Bailey," she whispered.

"Yeah, I'm here," Jackson said.

"You're not Bailey," Cassie slurred.

"We have to get out of the van," Jackson said. "I'm pinned beneath you. The van's on fire."

"I can't feel anything. I'm so cold," Cassie said.

"The van's on fire," Jackson said again. "Get me out of here. I didn't do anything to you people. I don't deserve this."

"Where's Bailey?" She began to move, but very slowly. She was so bloody.

"Get us out and we can help him," Jackson said. He would have said *anything* to get to safety.

Then she sort of threw herself toward the van door and fell out onto the ground. Jackson was freaked out by the smears of blood all over him. His neck was throbbing and his shoulders hurt as if someone was pulling them out of their sockets. Grinding his teeth in agony, he inched his way out through the doorway and fell next to Cassie, who sprawled with her arms and legs bent all wrong, inert.

"Get up," Jackson said, forcing himself to his knees. He looked down at her as he struggled to his feet. Her eyes were glassy, half open. He didn't know if she was dead. The back of the van was engulfed in rolling orange and scarlet flames. The heat blistered his face.

"Help me," he shouted, pivoting in a circle.

"Bailey," Cassie said faintly. Then, flatly, "Jackson."

"Did you call 911?" Jackson asked her. She was lying in a pool of her own blood. Her phone was in his pocket. "Did you call them?" He didn't know if they would come if you couldn't actually tell them where you were. Did they have ways to track cell phones?

"Jackson, we have to save Bailey," she said.

Like hell, Jackson thought. *So he can kill us both?*

"Yeah, okay," he said. "Call 911 and we can do that."

"*We* have to save him," she insisted.

"We will. After you call 911," he repeated. "And we need to get the handcuff key. Do you know where it is?"

"Bailey," she said. Then her eyes fluttered shut.

"Jackson's phone is ringing," Damon reported. "He's not answering."

"We think my boyfriend's been kidnapped by these people," Lydia told the dispatcher. "He's Jackson Whittemore. They were robbing his house. Can you patch into his phone and find out where he is?"

"I'm sorry, but we don't have the ability to do that," the dispatcher said.

"But there's an app," Lydia said. "I can give you his user ID and password."

"I'm sorry, but we can't do that," the dispatcher said. "But please tell me everything you can about the kidnapping."

"I'm downloading Where's My Phone onto my phone," Damon reported. "It'll take a few minutes."

"Hurry," Lydia told Damon's phone. *"Please."*

"The units are on their way, miss," the dispatcher told her.

Beacon Hills
Six Years Ago

It was Thursday, two days before Wolf Moon. Derek's relatives had gathered in the Hale house for the reunion. Derek was in charge of moving out all the furniture and breakables in the underground chamber so that the werewolves among them could den together for the next few days and nights. Sleeping bags, air mattresses, and cots were brought in, and they would let their wolf sides out to savor the bonding. The chamber was festively decorated for the occasion with large stone vases containing bouquets of lilies, roses, and iris, traditional flowers of France. The evocative scent of rosemary, another native French plant, filled the room. On Saturday, Derek would challenge Josh in human form; then, after the moon rose, they would vie for status as wolves.

Still without a car, Derek had managed to wrangle his Uncle Peter's motorcycle from him, and he left the chamber with his helmet on his hip, preparing to ride to school.

Laura, who was driving the Subaru, was sipping coffee as she walked to the car.

"Do you think I should ask Dad about giving Kate the Bite?" Derek whispered, not wanting any of his relatives to overhear.

Laura shook her head. "It's too soon. You haven't known her long enough. Maybe next year." She sat down behind the wheel and set her coffee in the drink holder. Then she shut the door.

"You don't think it's going to last, do you," Derek said, poking his head through the open window.

His sister let out a sigh and cupped his cheek. People said they looked so much like each other that they could be twins.

"I think you're crazy in love with her," she replied. "I don't know if that's good or bad. She's human, but we have human family members. Maybe she's doing a cougar on you. I don't know," she added quickly, as he opened his mouth to protest. "But you are going to have to tell Dad about her soon. This is getting serious."

"I will," Derek promised.

He knew he should have told his father about Kate— he didn't call her Ms. Argent anymore—way before now. Maybe he should have requested permission before he'd given Kate the ring she now wore. It wasn't an engagement ring or anything like that, just a token of how he felt about her. It was gold-plated and set with green stones, the best he could afford when he still didn't actually have a job. His Uncle Peter had given him some money in return for running a few errands.

He rode to school, got through classes, then did his laps with Kate until she'd put in her lifeguard hours. And then he went home with her. Within minutes of closing the door, the only thing she wore was his ring. They fell into each others' arms and made soulful, passionate love. She had taught him how to please her, and he did everything imaginable to her. In return, she aroused him to such heights that he had to turn away to hide the glow in his eyes, the lengthening of his teeth. He wanted to make love with her as a werewolf; he dreamed of it constantly, even though what they did now was more pleasurable than he had ever imagined.

Spent and exhausted, they would drowse together, and Derek would hear the call of the moon. He longed to run with her beneath its glow. He would prop himself up on his elbow, running his fingertips along her hair, staring at her, choked with love.

"I love you, Kate," he would whisper, but only when she was fast asleep.

That night, he had planned to ask her if she was going to chaperone the homecoming dance. He never went to anything at school, but Laura did, and she had suggested that he attend stag. All her girlfriends wanted to hang out with him and she was tired of disappointing them. He figured it was Laura's way of trying to get him interested in girls his own age, even if they were human.

He would have said no on the spot, but if Kate went as a chaperone, then at least they could see each other. Derek didn't dance, but the thought of seeing her in a formal gown would make enduring all the rest of it worthwhile.

But Kate was asleep, and he didn't want to wake her. He got up, showered, and dressed. She was still fast asleep when he got on his motorcycle.

He was nearly all the way home when he realized he had forgotten his school backpack. He called her. There was no answer. He tried again. Finally he turned around and rode back. He hated to bother her, but he knocked on the door— he didn't have a key—and she didn't answer. He rang the bell, and waited. He lowered his hand, not sure what to do.

Then he smelled her strong, wonderful scent, and moved to her bedroom window, cracked slightly open. He slid it open farther, removed the screen, and crawled inside.

CHAPTER SEVENTEEN

Beacon Hills
Six Years Ago

In Randy Andy's Bar and Grill across the street from her apartment, Kate bought Mr. Harris, the chemistry teacher at Beacon Hills High, two more shots. The empties were lined up in front of him. He was a hard-drinking alcoholic. And he sure knew his fun facts about arson.

His love of Randy Andy's was precisely what had prompted her to rent her apartment. Though he hadn't seen her around school, she had quickly figured out that he was a man who could help her. She'd pinpointed him as someone who was weak. Someone who could be manipulated.

Someone she could use.

"So," she said, "let me go through this with you one more time." She described the process by which you could burn down a house and not get arrested for it. He had explained it all to her a few nights prior. He was so drunk right now she doubted he'd remember this conversation.

"Yes. Hypothetically, of course," he said, staring down at her cleavage. She was wearing her pendant, the ancient family heirloom commemorating their triumph over the Beast of Gévaudan.

"Want another drink?" she said after a beat.

"Oh," he said, jerking his head back up to her face. He nearly fell off the bar stool. "Sure."

She gestured to the bartender to order another shot. Then she pulled a wad of bills from her wallet and dropped them onto the bar. The cheap but sweet ring Derek had bought for her glinted in the subdued light in the bar. It was a little bit too big and she played with it while she toyed with Harris.

"I have to go home now," she told Harris. "You should probably call it a night soon, too."

"I'm so drunk," he informed her, his head lolling.

"Poor baby," she cooed as Harris's last shot of the evening was placed before him on the bar.

Then she left. As she crossed the street, she spied Derek walking out of her apartment with his backpack.

Walking through the front door.

The door that had been locked.

She froze. He'd broken into her place. She couldn't believe it.

So, had he known all along that she was playing for the other side? Was *he* playing *her*? Had he found anything incriminating? Was her plan blown all to hell?

As she watched from the shadowed porch of the bar, the

neon light casting pastels over Derek like a lightly woven blanket, he got on his motorcycle, kicked it, and zoomed out onto the street.

Weighing various possibilities, she waited until he was out of sight. Then she darted across the street and jumped into her car. She drove after him, maintaining a safe distance as she followed him through the city of Beacon Hills, then up behind the preserve. The Hale house loomed in the darkness beneath the nearly full moon. Wolf Moon, on Saturday. There were cars everywhere. Full house, that Hale house.

Unwilling to get to close to the house, Kate parked and crept through the trees with a pair of binoculars. She followed Derek's progress as he entered a door set in the earth beneath the house. That would be the basement, the place where they congregated for special occasions, or used when their young wolf cubs couldn't control the shift. Shadows were moving around. So the family had moved down there for Wolf Moon. Nice. All she had to do was lock that entrance tight as a drum and throw in a few firebombs. She and her partners would douse the house proper, and ensure that all the Hales—werewolves or not—were taken care of.

Kate waited for a while to see if Derek raised some kind of alarm, which would indicate that he had found something in her house that had tipped him off to her plan. But the house and the werewolf den stayed dark.

Kate drove back to her place, body thrumming with the thrill of the chase. It was on. Without realizing it, Derek had thrown down the gauntlet, set the play in motion. If she found anything back at her apartment indicating that Derek knew about her plan, she'd cancel the operation, pack, and leave.

After she parked, she opened the door and hurried inside, to find a note from him on her entry table.

Dear Kate,

I left my backpack here and you weren't home. The window in your bedroom was slightly open and I came in that way. I put the screen back and walked out through the front door, but I made sure it was locked. I hope you don't mind. I won't do it again. It's just that all my homework was in the pack.

~~Lo~~ Yours,
Derek

She breathed a huge sigh. That had been very careless of her. She took note that he had begun to write *Love* and changed it to *Yours*. Sweet, unsure Derek. She was about to free him from his unending teenage angst.

By then, it was almost time for her late-night appointment, the last of her busy night. His name was Garrison Meyers, and he was an arson investigator. Kate's associates had authorized her to pay him a huge sum of money to declare that the fire at the Hale house they were about to set had been caused by an electrical wiring malfunction.

The fire had been planned for Saturday before dawn. But Derek's unexpected appearance in her house had scared her badly enough for her to want to get it done as fast as possible.

While she waited for Meyers, she placed a call on her cell phone.

"Dawn," she said. "Tomorrow. We're not waiting."

She got the answer she expected, and hung up.

The doorbell rang. Meyers had arrived.

It's showtime, she thought.

And smiled.

Dawn the next day.

It was not yet light out when Kate stopped at the gas station to fill up her gas can. She wanted to douse something with it—maybe the Alpha—and strike the match herself. She wanted—*needed*—to watch one of the Hales go up in flames the good, old-fashioned way, by her own hand. Maybe it was foolhardy to expose herself like that, but after the fire, she would be long gone.

She did take the precaution of going into the minimart to pay for the fuel with cash, rather than paying at the pump with her card. The man behind the counter was on his cell phone and he looked pissed off.

"I *told* you, I get paid *next* week," he said impatiently. "Jeez, Melissa, I get fired, and you complain. I get a job and you complain." He listened a moment. "Scott doesn't even need that damn inhaler," he went on. He saw Kate. "I gotta go. I have a customer."

He hung up.

Just another fine specimen of manhood, Kate thought. *Wouldn't it be lovely to be married to someone like this guy?*

"Hey, McCall," a man said. "I'll get that. Some guy's having problems with the car wash again. Go check it."

McCall made a face and muttered, "Why do I have to do it?" but came around the counter and went out the front door in disgust. The man turned to Kate, looked her up, looked her down. He was wearing a white shirt with Alan Seber engraved on a cheap plastic nameplate.

She put down thirty bucks and Alan Seber got her change. Then she hustled into her car and took off. Her pulse began to race, her heart to pound. She couldn't wait to see that house go up.

As she punched on some bouncy music, she replayed some of the finer moments of the crazy, no-holds-barred sex she and Derek had had. She couldn't deny she'd miss that. No one knew she'd slept with the enemy. They'd be shocked—revolted—if they found out. But she loved the danger. Derek had been a virgin, and a werewolf going through puberty, and she'd seduced him and taunted and lured him to do a full shift. He never had. Impressive. There were sixty ways she could have ended up dead— except for the Taser she kept under her pillow. And the weapons she'd hidden all over her house—under the couch, in the kitchen, and the bathroom. The risk had been huge. But that was what had made the sex so fantastic.

She looked down at the ring he had given her. Her lips

twitched, and then she began to laugh. She laughed all the
way to the Hale homestead.

The killing fields.

Was that Kate? Derek wondered as he came out of the bathroom at the minimart. He had his earbuds in, listening to
Wolfgang Gartner, so he hadn't quite picked up the voices
of the customer and the bored store clerk. Of course, he was
so in love with Kate that he heard her voice *everywhere.* He
thought every other woman he saw was her.

He and Laura were driving into school together super
early so Laura could attend her homecoming dance com-
mittee meeting. Her friends had agreed to hold it before
school so she could participate. She couldn't do it after
school today because the pack would begin its Wolf Moon
celebration, and the excuse Laura had given was that family was visiting from out of town. Very true. And since
Derek couldn't swim after school, either, their dad had
ordered Derek to leave the motorcycle at home and ride
with his sister.

Derek didn't know how he would be able to stand an
entire weekend without seeing Kate. He loved Wolf Moon
and all that came with it, but he loved Kate Argent, too.
Maybe this time next year she would get the Bite.

He knew Kate only lifeguarded in the afternoons, but
after Laura parked and went off to her meeting, he went to
the pool and watched the water shimmer. He could almost

see her swimming like a mermaid beside him. He wanted to howl of his devotion to her. Instead he walked to the pool's edge, dipped in his fingertips, and smiled.

Then he took advantage of the spare time to lift some weights in the gym. Surrounded by sweaty jocks, he silently pumped iron, reminding himself to hold back so he wouldn't betray how superstrong he was. He was going to kick Josh's ass in the challenge.

Derek showered, dressed, and entered the main corridor of the school. A freshly painted banner announcing the sale of homecoming dance tickets hung across the front door, where students were pouring in. He'd never been to a school dance before, and he was actually looking forward to it.

She's opening up my world, he thought. *She is my world.*

And then he heard Laura screaming.

Beacon Hills
The Present

"You can't trust human women," Derek murmured as he and Stiles stared into the campfire. The big bad wolfman had been silent for a long time, and Stiles wasn't sure where his mind had gone. Before Stiles could ask Derek if he'd like to share his story with the class—being him—Derek abruptly stood.

"I'm going to look some more," he said.

"Right. I'm good to go," Stiles affirmed, but as he scrambled to get up, he looked around and realized Derek had ditched him. He was already gone, charging back into the woods.

"Arghgrrwoww," Stiles muttered, imitating werewolf displeasure as best he could. He hunkered down to be useless and was about to play some more Wolfenstein on his phone—you had to love the classics in part because they were so ironic—when he heard a ding and jumped half a foot. Scott had texted him. Plus pictures. He looked at them. Cliff. Yow. Bushes.

Hmm.

"Derek!" Stiles shouted into the woods. "Scott checked in!"

There was no answer.

"Damn it, Derek. You *know* what you're getting for Christmas, right? A cell phone. So don't devour the Claus when he comes down that chimney," Stiles grumbled.

Stiles made the command decision to head off in Scott's direction. He would feel a million times better with some backup, but maybe Derek would hear him and close the distance.

On my way, Stiles texted back to Scott.

Derek heard Stiles yelling that he had found Scott, which was fine. And also nothing to do with him. Scott wasn't his priority at the moment.

The Alpha went this way.

He had caught the scent and was on the hunt. Tracking through the dense woods, he allowed himself to shift, then fell down onto all fours to close the distance between him and the Alpha. His hackles rose and he let himself howl.

Adrenaline and testosterone washed through his wolfish body and ignited his aggressive instincts. He was so close he could nearly taste the Alpha's blood.

I've got you now, he thought.

The Alpha.

Through the hazy smoke above them, Scott sensed the werewolf that had bitten him. The monster that had changed his life and was trying to force him into even more extreme changes.

His waking, walking nightmare.

Scott felt as if he had been plunged into ice, and he shivered, hard. The wolf inside Scott howled *crisis, menace, threat*; but it also cried *pack, belonging, Alpha.*

He tilted his head and allowed his eyesight to shift, keeping his face hidden from Allison as she cuddled in his arms for warmth. At the top of the cliff, a black shape moved like liquid among the boulders and trees. Then, in a heart-stopping moment, the Alpha's red eyes gazed down on Scott.

Scott almost threw up. Flashes of the terrible night when the Alpha had tried to make him kill Mr. Meyers shot through his mind like a strobe light. In his nightmarish memories, he had seen himself mauling Allison, hobbling her, dragging her down the length of the bus. It was what the Alpha wanted him to do, was willing him to do this very moment.

I didn't kill for you, Scott silently told the Alpha. *And I never will.*

But the memory of last night's dream was even fresher, and more real.

A wolf had appeared to him in his dream, and in real life.

"There's so much smoke," Allison said, waving her hand in front of her face. "I wonder if someone's campfire got out of control."

And there was fire.

In his dream.

And in real life.

Scott didn't answer. He was on the verge of shifting. He could feel the wolf inside him straining to come out for the Alpha. Or was it at the Alpha?

I hate you, Scott thought, but part of him quailed.

He hated the Alpha with all his heart.

And feared him with all his soul.

Then suddenly, an entire tree engulfed in flames rolled off the top of the cliff and crashed into the tiny horseshoe shape where Scott and Allison were huddled. Allison's scream was eclipsed by the massive crash and splintering as chunks of burning wood and sparks cascaded into the air, then showered down on them.

"Allison!" Scott shouted, throwing himself over her. Little fiery bombs smacked against him, and his clothes began to smolder.

"Scott, Scott!" Allison cried.

She pounded on his back and arms to put him out, then began pulling his jacket off of him. He helped her, checking his hair and hers. His shirt came next, and he whirled around, naked from the waist up, glaring at the spot where he had seen the Alpha. He sensed that it was still there, still watching. Waiting.

It wanted him to shift. But if he did, he would hurt Allison.

"Scott, Scott!" Allison cried as the tree blazed, flames taking up nearly all the room the two of them had been sharing. He fought the shift, squinting at the impenetrable thicket of bushes. It was the only way out—but he couldn't make himself go.

Allison's face was getting shiny and red; sweat was pouring across his biceps and pecs. He wished he could carry her out of there—

—and then he had a thought. If he could get the fire to ignite the bushes and burn some of them away, maybe she could escape. Maybe he could, too.

It's my dream, my horrible dream, he thought, as his nails began to lengthen and his teeth to sharpen. But he reminded himself that at the end of the dream, he had survived. And the real wolf had come. The real wolf had meant safety.

He didn't have time to figure out symbols and portents. He had to save Allison . . . and himself. Darting to the massive tree, he broke off one of the as-yet unburned limbs, dipped its leafy end into the fire, and tossed it at the bushes.

"What are you doing?" Allison cried.

"Trying to making a clearing," he said. "Then you can get out."

She watched him for a second. Then she reached forward to grab a branch, but more of the tree ignited with a loud *fwum*. She jumped away, colliding with Scott, who grabbed her and held her. In the scarlet firelight, he saw that his fingernails were growing longer.

This is what you want, he accused the Alpha silently. *But you can't have it. Ever.*

He eased her aside, grabbed another burning branch, and lobbed it in the same direction as the first one. All his hours of lacrosse drills paid off, as he hit the same section of bushes.

Allison burst into a fit of coughing. Doubling over, she hacked and choked, and she sounded like she was dying.

"I can't breathe, Scott," she said hoarsely. "There's too much smoke."

CHAPTER EIGHTEEN

Jackson looked down at the blur in his vision that was Cassie. She wasn't going to wake up anytime soon, and the fire from the van was creeping through the grass toward her. He didn't know what to do. He could try to bend backward and grab an arm or a leg, but he didn't think he could do it. He was seeing double, triple, and he could barely stand up.

If I could somehow yank off these cuffs, he thought.

He lurched away from the van, woozy and sick, forcing one leg in front of the other.

Then he heard her call softly, "Help."

Maybe a hero could do it. Maybe a hero would do it.

But as for Jackson, he staggered away as far as he could get, and then he collapsed onto the ground.

Scott put his arms around Allison, who was beginning to droop. He was coughing, too, and remembering what it felt like to be an asthmatic. Horrible. Life-ending. If she couldn't get some air, she would die.

It crossed his mind once to give her the Bite, but he didn't know if it would work. He was just a Beta.

Maybe that was what the Alpha had wanted him to do. He didn't know.

But he did know it wasn't the answer. Not here. Not now.

He let his vision go to red and saw that the section of bushes in front of them had been burned down until they were only chest high, if that tall. Allison had told him that she'd done gymnastics, and that gave him an idea.

"Allison," he said. "Listen. I'll get you on my shoulders and walk you over. Can you jump over the bushes then, and get out of here?"

"What about your ankle?" she asked.

"I can do it. I'll do it," he insisted.

"I can't leave you here," she said. Her voice sounded weak. Could she do it? Was this too crazy?

"We'll both die if you don't," he said.

Tears and sweat rolled down her face as she nodded. He got down on one knee. Clumsy from lack of oxygen, Allison struggled to climb up him like a circus performer.

He walked her over. The fire behind him was superhot. His body responded to the threat: his heartbeat shot up and he continued wolfing, quickly, and he realized that this was Allison's only chance. The fire wasn't high, or intense, where he walked her. But if she didn't get away from him, get away . . . away . . .

Up she went, and over, crashing into untouched vegetation. But smoke was pouring over it, and she emerged from a river of billowing gray just as he turned around, hunching his shoulders so that she wouldn't see.

"Scott! Maybe I can drag you out!" she cried.

"Go!" he ground out. "Please, Allison, go!"

Then more of the bushes burst into uncontrollable flame, and Scott was nearly surrounded.

And as Allison raced for help, he threw back his head and howled.

Stiles heard the howl.

Was that Scott? That was Scott! Is Scott in trouble? Is he eating someone up? Is someone eating him up? Is it the Alpha? Am I going to die now?

He followed his phone, shouting, "Derek! Scott! Derek! Scott!" as he zigzagged through the trees. He loved his phone. His good phone. He wanted it to keep working. It showed Scott's battery at 3 percent, but it showed it.

"Derek!" he bellowed.

"Yeah," Derek said, bursting from the trees. He was wolfed out, and Stiles let fly with a high-pitched, girly scream.

"Was that you?" Stiles yelled.

"No, that was you," Derek said in disgust.

"I mean the howl."

"It was Scott," Derek said. "In trouble. And I think I've caught the Alpha's scent."

"Oh, God," Stiles cried. They were running into what appeared to be a fog bank, but it was smoke. Stiles began to cough.

"The Alpha doesn't want to hurt Scott," Derek reminded him. "He needs him."

"But he doesn't need Allison," Stiles said, coughing, "and they're together."

"I don't need Allison, either," Derek muttered.

"I heard that," Stiles informed him in a choking voice.

"I don't care," Derek said.

There was smoke everywhere, but Stiles held out the phone so Derek could superwolf it with his special X-ray vision. "Look at those pictures," he said. "Cliff. Bushes."

"That looks like Cascade mountain ash," Derek said.

"And . . . we . . . care . . . why?" Stiles said as he began to cough harder and tire. He was a lacrosse player, which meant he had *some* endurance, but Derek was a freakin' machine.

"It's a kind of wood. It forms a barrier," Derek said.

Stiles didn't understand, but at the moment, he didn't care. He just wanted to get the two of them to Scott.

"Over there," Derek said, pointing.

Stiles and Derek clambered down from the path to a large group of boulders. Thick smoke was rising into the sky. Surely someone had seen it. Scrambling over the rocks, Stiles stared down the cliff.

Flames crackled from row upon row of bushes, rushing up their center branches and igniting the drooping canopies overhead. A tree had fallen to the base of the cliff. Scott had completely wolfed, and he was throwing himself frantically against a tiny piece of the sheer cliff not blocked by the blazing tree.

"Find handholds!" Stiles shouted.

"He can't hear you," Derek said grimly.

"Of course he can. He's a werewolf," Stiles insisted. "He can hear great!"

"No, I mean, he can't make sense of what you're saying. When a young werewolf is panicked like this, he's in pure survival mode. His instinct is to run. But there's nowhere for him to go."

"He doesn't know that," Stiles said. "Look."

Scott was mindlessly throwing himself against the wall over and over. Bits of rock were breaking free. Scott batted at them in rage as if they were intentionally attacking him. Then he flung himself backward against the cliff and howled at the flames.

"He's going to burn to death!" Stiles cried.

"He might," Derek said. "Do you have any rope in your Jeep?"

"In my Jeep?" Stiles said, doing a double take. "Derek, my Jeep's too far away, even for you."

Derek sniffed at the air. "Those bushes are definitely mountain ash," he said. "It's impenetrable to our kind. That's what trapped Scott there in the first place."

Stiles called up a map of the preserve and jabbed at the faceplate of his phone. "Look. There's a service road just beyond the mountain ash. They could get a fire engine in there. They could put it out and Scott goes home."

"No. No one can see him like this. Not when he's

shifted," Derek said, clenching his jaw as he studied Scott and his surroundings.

"And you're willing to let him burn to death instead?" Stiles said, covering his mouth against the smoke.

Derek was silent. Then he said through clenched teeth, "I'll ask again. Do you have any rope?"

"The rope will burn up," Stiles managed to say.

Derek turned glowing eyes his way. "Do. You. Have. Any. Rope?"

"What about the Alpha?" Stiles said. "Didn't you say he's nearby?"

Derek hesitated. "He won't hurt me, either," he said.

Stiles shook his head. "You don't sound sure enough. I don't care what you say," Stiles said, although of course he did. He way did. "I'm calling 911."

"No!" Derek yelled, swinging at Stiles.

And to Stiles's amazement, he ducked in time. And then he pushed Derek, hard. Derek staggered backward against a couple of the boulders. They gave way, and they and Derek fell over the cliff.

"Oh, my God!" Stiles shouted.

Derek landed hard on his back and went limp. The boulders just missed hitting him, and he was so winded he didn't even move out of their way. He was still in human form, and his head was dangerously close to an outcropping of blazing tree branches. So many times, Stiles had wished for Derek to up and die. But he hadn't meant for him to really die.

Except that he *had* meant for him to really die. Just maybe not in pain, and not in front of Stiles.

Then Scott howled and flung himself on top of Derek like a rabid dog.

Stiles cupped his hands and yelled down to Scott. "Scott, Scott!" he shouted. "No! Bad wolf!"

Scott didn't even look up at him. Crouching on Derek's chest like some nightmare, he threw his head back, howled, and dove toward Derek's throat—

—just as Derek snapped out of it and wolfed.

"Yes!" Stiles shouted, then realized what he was doing—cheering that Derek had just turned into something that could rip out Scott's guts and barbecue them. Derek howled at Scott and grabbed him around the throat as he leaped to his feet. He tossed Scott backward against the cliff as if Scott were a rag doll. Stunned, Scott slid down, his legs splayed.

Then after a second, Scott sprang at Derek and Stiles yelled, "Oh, my God! Oh, my God!" and coughed up his lungs as Derek stood his ground. If Derek had moved so much as six inches left or right, Scott would have soared into the fire. But Scott wasn't reasoning. He didn't know that.

Derek punched Scott backward against the cliff again. Stiles wondered if Derek could just throw him up to the top of the cliff.

"Werewolf toss," he shouted down to Derek. "I'll try to catch him."

But Derek had fallen to one knee, obviously winded, maybe hurt. Scott lay on his side, panting.

A wind washed through the tops of the bushes and showered Derek with fiery debris, setting his jacket on fire.

Still in wolf face, Derek flung himself to the dirt, rolling around, then ripped off the jacket in shreds, bringing his shirt with it. Like Scott, he was naked from the waist up.

Then Scott staggered back up to his feet. He, too, was still wolfed out.

"Think about Allison!" Stiles yelled down to him. Sometimes that brought him out of his wolf berserkness. "Allison, Allison, Allison!"

There was no sign in Scott's glowing golden eyes that he knew what Stiles was saying. Stiles groaned and blew the air out of his cheeks.

"Screw it," he said. He dialed 911.

"Nine-one-one, what is your emergency?" said a familiar voice. Stiles knew all the dispatchers.

"Hey, it's me, Stiles, there's a fire," Stiles said.

"Stiles, no!" Derek shouted up to him.

Stiles ignored him. He wasn't going to stand there and watch his best friend burn to death. He could only hope and pray that Scott would be able to transform back before the firefighters came. Maybe the pain would snap him out of it. That was what Derek said would keep him human. Pain.

Down in a fire pit? Plenty of that.

"Beacon Hills Preserve," Stiles said when the dispatcher asked him for his location. "The south side. There's a service road in, and once the trucks—and I mean trucks, plural—get here you'll see exactly what I mean."

He hung up. All the calls were recorded. Somehow his father might hear that call and know he'd made it, but that was the least of his concerns at the moment. Scott was not coming out of it. He launched himself at Derek, again, who was obviously feeling the burn.

Allison charged through the woods, calling for help. Which way to the road? There was smoke everywhere, and her eyes were watering; but she was also crying because she wouldn't be able to get help for Scott in time and he would die.

She stumbled over a root and went down, hard. Panting, she pushed herself up to her hands and knees.

And felt something looming over her. Something breathing on her. An animal.

An evil animal.

Death.

She hitched gasps and coughs as she shut her eyes tightly. She was terrified. Hot breath condensed on the back of her neck. The thing was coming closer, closer . . .

"Scott," she whispered.

The thing seemed to stop.

And then the feeling left, as if the animal had moved away. Exhaling a sob, she lifted her head.

The wolf that she and Scott had seen that morning was standing about ten feet away from her, watching her. She froze, staring at it.

Then it turned around and disappeared into the trees. Stunned, she stood up painfully. Her ankle seized. Now it was her turn to have a sprain. Just when they didn't need any more problems.

Still, she could put weight on it . . . and she hobbled forward, then stopped, reaching out and snapping off a branch from a tree. Which way to go?

"I need help," she murmured aloud, planting the stick beside herself for support.

The wolf reappeared. Gazing at her, it half turned and looked over its shoulder at her. She stayed motionless, breathless.

It turned and faced her, and stared at her.

"What?" she asked. "What do you want?"

It kept looking at her. Then it backed up, turned around, and looked at her over its shoulder again.

"Do you want me to follow you?" she said.

It started walking. Allison squared her shoulders and wrapped her hand tightly around the stick. The wolf glided forward. Keeping her distance, she followed behind, bracing herself in case it turned on her, or led her into an ambush of hungry wolves waiting for prey. All she had was a stick, but at least she had that.

They hadn't gone very far before she saw that they were on a hill overlooking a wide road—another way into the preserve. Her heart soared and she let out a sob of joy.

The wolf looked at her, turned tail, and trotted away. Allison half slid, half crawled down to the road, everything in her praying for someone to come by. The smoke was so thick—surely someone had called in the fire. Fire trucks must be on their way.

She waved her arms at an approaching car, but it just swerved around her and continued on. Allison had to stagger out of the way or it might have hit her. Swallowing down a strangled sob of frustration, she staggered back to the side of the road and waited for another car to drive by. Then she heard sirens, and she caught her breath and held onto the stick with both hands for support, whispering, "Thank you thank you thank you."

A few minutes later, a red Beacon Hills fire truck roared by, followed by an ambulance. Then, to her surprise, her aunt's car trailed after the emergency vehicles.

"Aunt Kate!" she shouted, though of course her aunt couldn't hear her.

She dashed back into the road and waved her arms. Her aunt honked her horn once and angled over toward her, screeching to a stop and unrolling her window.

"Allison, what the hell are you doing here?" she yelled.

"Please, let's go, please," Allison said, jerking open the passenger door behind her aunt. She fell in and her aunt put on the turbo almost before Allison had a chance to shut the door.

Fearfully she glanced out the window at the clouds of smoke. Then she saw the wolf keeping pace with the car as it darted through the trees, its gaze steadily on her.

"What are you doing out here?" Aunt Kate said again. "You're supposed to be with Lydia."

"I heard about the fire and I came to see," she said, hearing her voice crack. Her aunt would probably know she was lying, but right now she didn't care. "Please, have you heard if Scott's okay?"

"How did the fire get started?"

"I don't know," Allison said desperately.

"Why didn't you drive out of it? Why are you on foot?"

Why so many questions? Allison wanted to shout. But she

knew her aunt was asking because she cared about her. "I dropped my keys," she said. "I got a call from Scott and I ran to the fire and then I panicked and I—I couldn't find them." She started crying. "Oh, God, he's stuck down there. He hurt his ankle and he couldn't get out."

"It'll be okay," her aunt said calmly. "The fire department's on its way."

Allison nodded and stared out the window at the wolf, which could no longer keep up with the car. It stopped, and Allison watched it grow smaller and smaller as Kate drove on down the road.

The van exploded, and Jackson stagger-walked. He didn't turn to look. He didn't want to see. How hard had he tried to save Cassie?

What could I have done? he asked himself. *I had to get out of there.*

Then the scream of sirens filled the smoke-choked air and Jackson lurched toward them. A sharp wind thinned the clouds of gray for a moment and he let out a harsh, sharp laugh when he caught sight of the preserve parking lot. Police cars were roaring into it, and was that Danny's Lexus?

Jackson collapsed.

CHAPTER NINETEEN

Derek could hear the fire trucks coming, but Scott hadn't shifted back to human form. He was still fighting Derek, howling and grunting, in full werewolf form. The fire was raging around them, and there was too much mountain ash to cross anywhere. The cliff was too high.

Then he saw the boulders that he'd knocked down when he'd fallen. If he and Scott could push them into the bushes and crush them, they might be able to cross over on top of the rocks.

"Scott," he said, "listen to me. Listen."

Scott grunted and howled. Derek wondered if the time had come, if finally he would have to sacrifice Scott to maintain their secret. He'd thought about it many times, and used the threat to try to talk Scott out of behaving rashly. Once or twice it had actually worked. But not usually.

"Scott," he tried again. He slapped Scott hard across the face. "If you don't shift, Allison will never see you alive again."

Scott showed his sharp fangs in utter rage.

"Allison," Derek said to him.

Scott cocked his head. Staggered backward. Nearly fell into the funeral pyre that was the tree, and then, miraculously, shifted.

"Derek?" he said, running his hands through his hair, slicking it back. "What happened?" He dropped his arms to his sides and looked around. "Did Allison make it out?"

"Yes," Derek said. "And we've got a chance, too."

He explained his plan to Scott. Together they got on one side of the largest boulder—perilously close to the fire—and pushed it forward, into the burning mountain ash. It was heavy, and as they grunted, searing welts and blisters rose on Scott's back. Inch by inch, they shoved it into the vegetation. It smothered the flames and they hoped it would provide a shield between them and the bushes.

Derek climbed up the boulder. He felt himself begin to shift back into werewolf form as he bent down and held out his hand to Scott. As Scott grabbed it, Derek's fingernails grew and sliced into Scott's wrist.

And Scott saw:

Laura heard about it first, when the principal came to get her. And they drove them there, someone drove them.

And Derek could see it as if he'd been there, saw it all, felt it all in his soul as the house smoked and the bodies were gone. The screams and the cries and the shouts and the little ones burning.

Laura seeing it all as she and Derek stood in the ashes of their smoldering home. The Hale siblings insane with grief, but not shifting, because the fire trucks were there and the EMTs were there. And even their grief was stolen from them.

They wheeled out Uncle Peter, and Derek held Laura's head

away so she wouldn't see the horror he had become. He'll probably die, they told the two Hale kids. We're so sorry, we're sorry; we'll get to the bottom of this.

Laura, crazy, screaming, "Who did this? Who could do this?"

But she knew it had to be hunters.

And as she sank to into the charred ruins in her brother's arms, Derek saw the glint of metal in the wreckage. A melted gold ring, with little green stones. Had it slipped off by accident? Or had she taken it off her finger and let it drop into the fire? Did she want him to find it? Had she wanted him to know?

He stared at it for a lifetime, for an eternity; then he picked it up and put it in his pocket.

Tears slid down his face.

For days.

And then they hardened like the molten pools of metal in the foundation of his home.

Jackson was on his way to the hospital in an ambulance. When Lydia was told that she wasn't family and therefore would not be allowed to ride with him, she ignored the EMT and climbed inside. She simply said no each time he insisted that she come out.

Jackson was quiet. He kept thinking about Cassie. He'd overheard the deputy talking to Sheriff Stilinski on the radio. Cassie had tried to crawl away, but the fire had overtaken her.

What could he have done?

Nothing, he insisted. *I had to leave her there.*

The thieves at his house had been caught. The one Danny had hit with a lacrosse ball had a concussion.

And what about his biological father? The picture was still in his pocket. Had that been part of the scam? Or had Bailey Gramm's father really known Jackson's dad?

"You're in big trouble for everything you've done, and there's a small box of punishment in your dresser drawer," Lydia told Jackson. But you're going to be okay." And even thought he was a little confused, he smiled wryly, because her words weren't intended to comfort.

They were an order.

It seemed odd that Aunt Kate had just happened to be out driving when she'd seen the fire and decided to investigate. Several of the things Allison's family had told her lately didn't add up, and that felt like one more. But that wasn't important now.

Allison leaped out of her aunt's car before it had come to a full stop. Well away from the blaze, an ambulance was parked with its back door wide open. Framed by the light, Scott and Stiles were sitting together on the bumper. Scott was breathing into some kind of machine—oxygen mask—and he had a blanket around his shoulders. An EMT was patting a gurney, and Scott was shaking his head.

"Scott!" Allison cried. She ran to him, laughing and shrieking, saying his name over and over. He was alive. The fire was raging all over the preserve, and she'd been afraid she'd never see him again.

Both he and Stiles looked up and saw her. Rising unsteadily, Scott threw off the blanket and fumbled with the mask. She eased herself carefully against him, and began to cry.

"He's okay, Allison," Stiles said. "They're going to take him to the hospital so his mom can smack him upside the head about two dozen times. But after that, he's a free man."

"I think now we're busted," Scott rasped.

"I don't care. I don't care *forever*," Allison said, reaching out an arm and hugging Stiles, too.

"Ooph," Stiles said, pretending she had squeezed too hard. "My best estimate? You'll care in about an hour, once the euphoria has worn off." Then, as Allison carefully kissed Scott on the lips, and Scott pulled her against his chest, Stiles said, "Or . . . you won't care ever."

Derek sat farther away, on the back of a fire truck, and his gaze moved from the happy trio to Kate Argent as she ambled behind her niece. They locked gazes, and she smiled at him. Gave him a wink.

"Seems like old times," she said. "Doesn't it, lover?"

Then she turned and walked away, joining the others.

Derek studied her with the eyes of a predator, and burned with such hatred that he was practically on fire.

And somewhere, not too far away, the howl of a wolf echoed in the night. The howl was a promise:

There are more of us, bent on payback. And domination. And death.

And we are coming.